"She's Harry Potter without a wand; Katniss Everdeen without a quiver. It's the world against Arcadia, armed only with her fabulous, prodigious, logical mind. A super impressive debut."

Tony Wilson, author of *Stuff Happens: Jack*

"Chesterman's compelling creation of Arcadia, a preternaturally precocious sleuth with an unsettlingly clear-sighted and plain-spoken manner, is matched by the twists and turns of a devious plot, making for a true page-turner."

Philip Jeyaretnam, S.C., lawyer and author of *Abraham's Promise*

"Packed with intellectual puzzles, the taut chain of events invites the reader's participation every step of the way. This subtle, intriguing novel raises the bar for young adult contemporary fiction. When we enter the world of our brilliant teenage protagonist with all its attendant mysteries—who is Arcadia? Who is our killer?—we are reminded that the present, viewed keenly, holds all the keys to the past. This book is impossible to put down."

Michelle Martin, radio personality and host of *Talking Books*

"*Raising Arcadia* is a pacy mystery novel that has, at its centre, the irrepressible (and perhaps sociopathic) heroine Arcadia, a sixteen-year-old searching for her place in the adult world. Stuffed with intrigue and mystery, it will be adored by young adults and by adults who prize curiosity and challenge. Read it—and then read it again, to see if you noticed all the clues."

Adrian Tan, lawyer and author of *The Teenage Textbook*

THE FINAL BOOK IN THE RAISING ARCADIA TRILOGY

SIMON CHESTERMAN

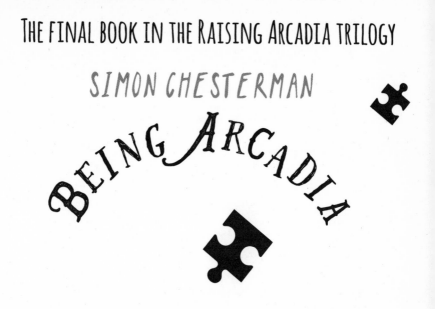

BEING ARCADIA

Marshall Cavendish
Editions

Published by Marshall Cavendish Editions
An imprint of Marshall Cavendish International

A member of the
Times Publishing Group

Other Marshall Cavendish Offices:
Marshall Cavendish Corporation. 99 White Plains Road, Tarrytown NY 10591-9001, USA •
Marshall Cavendish International (Thailand) Co Ltd. 253 Asoke, 12th Flr, Sukhumvit 21 Road,
Klongtoey Nua, Wattana, Bangkok 10110, Thailand • Marshall Cavendish (Malaysia) Sdn Bhd,
Times Subang, Lot 46, Subang Hi-Tech Industrial Park, Batu Tiga, 40000 Shah Alam, Selangor
Darul Ehsan, Malaysia.

Marshall Cavendish is a registered trademark of Times Publishing Limited

National Library Board, Singapore Cataloguing in Publication Data
Names: Chesterman, Simon.
Title: Being Arcadia / Simon Chesterman.
Description: Singapore : Marshall Cavendish Editions, [2017] | Series: Raising Arcadia ; book 3.
Identifiers: OCN 993102385 | 978-981-4751-52-0 (paperback)
Subjects: LCSH: High school girls--Fiction. | England--Fiction. | Detective and mystery stories.
Classification: DDC 828.99343--dc23

Printed in Singapore by Fabulous Printers Pte Ltd

For N

CONTENTS

PROLOGUE

It begins as a flicker.

Light dances with the shadows, moving as I move. There is no sound, no crackling. No smoke.

I turn in slow motion, a duet with the orange tongues that now lap at my dress. Stop, drop, and roll? I am— I appear disoriented. Wandering this way and that, I only fan the tendrils that now climb up my back.

Hands over my face. Protecting it from heat but only delaying the inevitable. Still I move, unable to escape the incandescence that trails me like an aura. It is terrible; it is beautiful.

Until at last a primal scream erupts from my lips as the flames engulf me.

1
ESCAPE

"We don't have much time," says Henry—wasting some.

On the screen, numbers count down. One minute, thirteen seconds. Twelve seconds.

No wires to cut, no cheery ringtones today. The cylinder resembles a torpedo but lacks a propeller. Welded to the outside is a simple laptop, the liquid crystal display of which shows the task and the time remaining.

Not exactly what she has prepared for. But perhaps that is the point?

The screen also shows an icon in the shape of a trefoil—a stylised three-leaf clover. Similar to the one painted on the brushed steel of the cylinder, it is trimmed so that, instead of leaves, three equally-spaced wedges extend from a central circle. Black on yellow, it is the international symbol for a radiation hazard.

Hazard only means risk. Similar signs appear on x-ray machines around the world. Used properly, they are film-safe and person-safe. This device, however, if used properly would destroy most of Oxford.

She looks again at the puzzle on the screen.

$$16, 06, 68, 88, \_\_, 98$$

A number sequence problem, but not necessarily an arithmetic one. Minus ten, plus sixty-two, plus twenty, then what?

Based on 1940s technology, nuclear weapons are physics at its highest and its lowest. A chain reaction is the break-up of matter itself, heavier atoms like uranium decaying into lighter elements. As the bonds that once held the uranium together are broken, Einstein's famous equation comes to life as some of that mass becomes energy.

Why "06"? If it is read as "zero-six" it has three syllables, as do all the others except sixteen. Six-and-ten? Not specific enough; there are dozens of two-digit numbers with three syllables. Sixty-six, to be precise.

$E=mc^2$. Though the amount of mass lost is tiny, when multiplied by the square of the speed of light it tends to add up. Just one gram of mass is equivalent to around ninety thousand billion joules of energy—what twenty-five thousand homes might use in a year. The release of energy here would be in fractions of a second, however. A better measure is the destruction caused by the bomb that was dropped on Hiroshima at the end of the Second World War. That blast was the result of a mass-energy conversion of seven-tenths of one gram, about the weight of a raisin.

Could it have something to do with spelling? Each number uses the vowels "i" and "e".

"Should we just split the difference and put 93?"

Henry is trying to be helpful but she wrinkles her nose. Guessing offends her. "You're right that any answer is better than nothing," she says, "but this isn't meant to be chance. There is a correct answer if we can find it."

Thirty-seven seconds.

If a chain reaction represents the highest form of physics, getting it started is the lowest: critical mass is a fancy term for squashing the uranium into a ball dense enough that the splitting of one atom causes the breakup of another and so on. This can be done by positioning explosives around it, or simply ramming one piece of nuclear material into another. Compress the atoms enough and the chain reaction begins.

She looks more closely at the laptop. The keys have barely been used. Some fingerprints on the screen, but no hints there. The locked closet within which the bomb was hidden opened with a key they had retrieved from a drain using a flexible magnet. The magnet had in turn been found in a safe opened with a password generated by the page number of a Bible passage. And so on. Is this the last test? No, for the door of the hotel room remains locked.

"Come on, Arcadia," Henry is speaking again, "we have to try something."

She refuses to admit defeat. Try something, try anything. Sixteen, zero-six…

"I thought you could do this sort of thing standing on your head."

She tries to shut out his voice as the seconds tick down, clearing her mind for one last attempt to view the problem from every angle, when she sees her mistake.

"Once again, Henry"—she smiles for the first time—"you have saved our lives."

On the laptop keyboard she taps an "L" and then an "8". The timer stops at six seconds.

Henry looks at the screen, then her, in confusion. "What does that even mean?"

Above them she hears footsteps, leather-soled shoes on metal. "Nicely done, Miss Arcadia." Dr. Joseph Bell steps forward on the elevated walkway that runs the length of the fake hotel room. "You've made it further than anyone else today. Let's see if you can get past the final test."

It is the first time she has been back to Oxford in a year. Her previous visit also featured a bomb—in that case a real one that threatened the John Radcliffe Hospital, which serves as the university's medical school.

That was when she first met Dr. Bell, while searching for information about her birth. Her medical records show that she was born at the John Radcliffe, second child of Euphemia and John Hebron. A month later, the couple died in a car crash. She was adopted by the same family that had taken in their first child, her brother Magnus, seven years earlier.

Yet the Hebrons' own paper records make clear that they died childless. Dr. Bell himself signed the death certificates. When she discovered this, a phone call brought her to Dr. Bell's office; there she found him strapped to a bomb large enough to kill them both and destroy the hospital—removing any evidence of the deception and the only two people who knew about it.

And yet. That bomb was also a test, a means of evaluating her for— for what?

On this occasion, the "bomb" is the coda to a day of more subtle evaluation. Admission to Oxford University is notoriously opaque. Past and anticipated grades are considered, a personal statement is thrown in, but central to the alchemy is an interview with fellows of the college to which one applies. She once dined with some of those fellows and has yet to conclude whether that is an advantage or not. Having observed their alcohol-infused discussions at close range makes it difficult to maintain the proper reverence when being asked why she should be admitted into the hallowed halls.

Two days ago, her mathematics teacher, Mr. Aveling, was tasked with speaking to the Priory School's upper sixth students who had been selected for Oxford interviews. After some notes on practicalities and personal hygiene, his advice boiled down to two things: be brilliant—and don't let the school down.

And so on Tuesday she, Henry, and five other upper sixth students arrived at Oxford with overnight bags. Only she and Henry had applied to Magdalen College and were dropped off first when the school minibus pulled into the High Street. From the Porter's Lodge they were directed to small bedrooms on separate floors. A quick inspection revealed hers to have been abandoned hastily by an undergraduate student sent home at the end of term. He or she—from the state of the basin, definitely *he*—could do with some tips on personal hygiene.

Henry continues to think that he has a chance of being admitted into Oxford only because of his parents' money, an underestimation of his intellect that she finds endearing. Of more concern is that he might be applying to Magdalen only because that is where she applied. She avoids social media, but this is an occasion where the simple status update "it's complicated" might be apt. Set that thought aside for later consideration.

For her part, she has decided on Oxford because it is not Cambridge, where her brother spent so many years. Magnus has at last graduated and assumed a government position about which he takes undue pleasure in being mysterious. But the impression he left on Cambridge—metaphorical and literal—is significant; she has no desire to be seen in his plus-size shadow.

If she is honest with herself, the choice of Oxford was

also partly due to Dr. Bell's advice. Having nearly been blown up together forged a bond of a kind; he also tried to help her find out the truth about her parents. They have not seen each other since then, but six months ago he wrote her a letter in precise longhand, inquiring after her studies and suggesting that she consider Oxford in general and his college, Magdalen, in particular.

Why his advice resonated with her is unclear. It was more than the shared experience of the bomb, more than his help. Set that thought aside also for the time being.

After settling into their rooms they were given a tour of the college and then invited to dinner at Hall. On her previous visit she dined at High Table as a guest of Dr. Bell. Last night's fare was simpler: a mix of proteins, starches, and vegetables all apparently chosen for their different shades of yellow. She sat with Henry as other students milled about, sizing each other up and making half-hearted attempts at conversation that tended to focus on the public school one attended, with occasional gasps at encountering someone from a comprehensive.

The next morning two interviews were scheduled with tutors at the college. An ageless woman in a shapeless sweater asked her about organic chemistry. Then Lucian Smythe, one of the younger fellows whom she met on her previous visit, gave her a simple problem to solve concerning seven pirates who were to divide up gold according to some unlikely "pirate rules".

Each discussion was moderately interesting, yet she had

begun to reconsider whether the intellectual stimulation of an Oxford education was quite worth the hassle of its peculiar institutions and individuals. It was towards the end of lunch—the colour palette now extending to include orange—that Dr. Bell approached and asked if she and her friend might be willing to take part in an optional component of admissions that the college was trying out.

Refusal seemed churlish, so she and Henry accompanied him through the cloisters and onto a lawn on which a marquee had been erected.

"We are preparing for a Gaudy next week—a kind of party for former students of the college," Dr. Bell explained. "There is a feast and dancing in Hall, but there are also games, magic shows and so on and so forth."

He led them into the marquee, within which a stage had been built. But it was a stage without space for an audience, four walls enclosing a box in the middle of the oversized tent. A cheery sign on the only door read: "Welcome to the Hotel California". They stepped inside. It had indeed been decorated as a hotel room, approximately four metres square, complete with bed, closet, and washbasin. There was no ceiling, presumably the better to observe participants from the elevated walkway that ran along the top of one wall, reached via steps from outside the room.

"It's called an 'Escape Room'," Dr. Bell said at the time. "Apparently they're quite the thing in America these days. One has a certain amount of time and must solve puzzles and so on to escape, as it were. Some of our graduate students requested it for the Gaudy and then one bright spark asked if we could use it for admissions."

Dr. Bell sniffed. "I confess that I doubted whether it would be particularly useful as an admissions exercise, but we've had a handful of candidates try it out. Most fared rather poorly, I fear—I suspect the lateral thinking demanded throws off many of our narrower candidates."

The basin was not connected to a water supply, she observed. A picture hung on the wall too upright, probably hinged and possibly with a safe behind it. Symbols had been drawn on the plasterboard above the bed; the bed itself was covered with a quilt whose patchwork followed a complex sequence. Pi, as she later confirmed. There was an odd, sweet smell in the room.

"And then I recalled"—Dr. Bell was still speaking— "that you were rather good at puzzles. So would you be willing to give it a shot?"

⌘

"How is 'L-8' even an answer?" Henry protests.

She is already onto the next problem, but the fact that they are in this together suggests that teamwork is part of the "test". So she pauses to explain.

"Actually you gave me the answer yourself," she says. "Stand on your head and look at the problem."

Frowning, Henry crouches down and is about to put his head on the carpet.

"Not *literally*," she tuts. "Just imagine you were looking at the sequence upside down. '16, 06, 68, 88, __, 98' becomes '86, __, 88, 89, 90, 91'. So the answer is '87', which you can write upside down as 'L8'."

Henry's mouth forms a silent "O". She should be more generous: it was he who first worked out that the flexible magnet could reach down the drain of the washbasin and retrieve the key.

Now there is just one puzzle left. The storyline that Dr. Bell explained to them, setting up the game, was that they were secret agents seeking to disarm a nuclear bomb and then escape from the hotel room before enemy agents arrived. A somewhat implausible scenario, but justifying a series of challenges without requiring additional real estate.

Having dealt with the bomb, they must now work out how to leave the room. The symbols above the bed are the key:

The same symbols appear on five buttons next to the door, which is held shut by an electromagnetic lock. Adjacent to the buttons, an emergency release offers a simpler exit from the room—but concedes defeat in the game. Above the buttons are three lights.

Henry presses one button at random, earning a beep. He then presses a second, and a third. On the fifth button a buzzer sounds and the first light glows red. So, five buttons to press but in a precise order. The first of the three lights stays illuminated.

"I think that's enough guessing, Henry," she says. "We get three tries at this and that was the first."

On the walkway above them, she knows, Dr. Bell is smiling. He knows the solution and is seeing how long it takes her to work it out.

Five buttons. More than three thousand possible combinations, fewer—one hundred and twenty—if each button is to be pressed only once. But they only have two more attempts.

"I've got it!" cries Henry. "It's the number of straight lines. It goes from zero to one, then two, then four, then five." Triumphant, and before she can stop him, he presses the buttons in sequence:

$$8\ \heartsuit\ \overline{}\,\delta\ M\ A$$

A buzzer sounds twice; a second red light illuminates.

"Two strikes, Miss Arcadia," Dr. Bell intones above them. "You would do well to choose carefully next time."

She has also considered the straight lines briefly, and the number of angles, enclosed areas, and other geometric features. But the theme has been lateral thinking. What does it mean to think laterally? Adopting an indirect or creative approach, as opposed to solving a problem logically; looking at it from a different perspective? Edward de Bono made a small industry out of telling people to think using six coloured hats, each representing a different aspect from which a problem might be approached.

Yet "lateral" simply means from the side. So what would it mean to look at this question sideways?

Again she smiles, approaching the keypad.

"Arcadia," Henry says quietly, hesitating before stepping aside. "Are you sure you've got it? I mean, of course you're sure—but are you actually right?"

"You worry too much, Henry," she replies. She presses the buttons in the correct order:

$$M \heartsuit 8 \text{⧾} \text{♃}$$

Instead of a buzzer, the lock emits a single beep and the three lights turn green.

"Well done again, Miss Arcadia," Dr. Bell says. Seeing Henry's evident confusion, he adds: "Might you explain the solution to your friend? I thought it was a rather clever use of lateral thinking."

Henry is frowning at the symbols and holds up a hand. "Give me a second." Then he uses the same hand to slap himself in the forehead. "Of course—lateral thinking, sideways. Each of these figures is symmetrical, a mirror image of itself. Take the right half of each and you get 1, 2, 3, 4, 5."

She resists the urge to congratulate him as it will sound patronising. "Exactly," is all she says.

Gentleman that he is, Henry reaches forward to open the door for her and then his frown returns. It opened easily when they came in, but the magnetic lock has not disengaged. He leans against the door but it is solid wood and does not move.

"Is there a problem?" Dr. Bell enquires from his perch.

"The door release appears to be jammed," she replies, trying the handle herself. The lights above the button are shining a steady green but the door remains locked.

"Now that's odd," Dr. Bell says. He turns to pull a lever on the side of the walkway. There is the sound of a latch being released and the scrape of metal on metal as a narrow set of retractable stairs is lowered from the elevated platform. Gasping, he climbs down the steps, catches his breath, and then joins them at the door.

He pushes the buttons in the correct sequence once again. Again the lights glow green, there is a single beep, but the door remains locked.

"How strange," Dr. Bell murmurs to himself. "It has worked impeccably all day. Perhaps there is a bug in the system. Ah well." Sighing, he presses the emergency release and gestures for Henry to try the door.

The two-second alarm that rings covers the sound of footsteps on the metal walkway, but it fades before the clanking of the stairs being raised has subsided. Henry is still trying in vain to open the door when she taps him on the shoulder to turn around.

"What?" Henry says, looking at her and Dr. Bell before following their gaze up to the walkway. Colour drains from his face as he registers the person standing there. "Oh God, not again."

"Hello to you too, sweetie-pie. Did you miss me?" The voice is hers and yet not hers; accelerated slightly, like the movements of the figure, clad entirely in black, that now paces above them. The figure is also hers and not hers; the same shape but moving in jerks, twitches of nervous energy being released. The other her blows a kiss towards Henry, who shifts as if to dodge its impact.

"Hello, Moira," Arcadia says at last. "Long time no see."

She has met Moira only once before. On that occasion, her twin sister shot her with a tranquiliser dart, tied her to a chair, threatened to suffocate her with a plastic bag, and then pointed a loaded gun at her head. Apart from that, the encounter went well.

The other her grins. "Indeed! So, welcome to my Hotel California, Arky. If you had paid more attention to the song, you would have known that you can check out any time you like—but you can never leave."

It was Moira who strapped the bomb to Dr. Bell that almost blew up the John Radcliffe Hospital. Having escaped from the laboratory in which she was part of a genetic experiment, her plan had initially been to assume Arcadia's identity and remove any evidence of her own existence. On each occasion, however, she had given Arcadia a chance to cheat death, or to prove her worthiness. But worthiness for what?

"Not drinking today?" Arcadia asks. Keeping Moira in conversation seemed to rein in some of her more homicidal tendencies. At their previous meeting, the other her carried a bottle of fluids that she needed to drink regularly—electrolytes, beta-blockers, and something called DHA—or else her brain would begin to shut down. Eventually, she would die.

Moira taps her arm. "My variation on the nicotine patch. A slow release of all the goodies I need to start my day right. That and an apple a day keep the doctor away. But you have to throw the apple fairly hard." The other her laughs to herself. "It's always apples, isn't it, Dr. Bell?"

Dr. Bell is looking at her curiously. "Am I to understand," he says to Arcadia, "that this is the girl who nearly killed us a year ago? Your twin?"

"I didn't know she was my twin at the time," Arcadia replies.

"Oh, so we're playing it like that, are we?" Moira interrupts. "You know, Arky, they say the Devil's greatest trick is persuading you that he doesn't exist. The problem is that people are so gullible. Just think how dim the average person is—and half of them are even dumber than that!"

Why is Moira here, why now? After the aborted—or abandoned—attempts to kill Arcadia a year ago, the other her disappeared. On the same day, one of the scientists who ran the laboratory in which Moira had been imprisoned died when his car exploded. Though there was clearly foul play, the police have no leads as to who killed Lysander Starr or why. It is possible that Moira had planted the bomb—she certainly had a motive—but a simple detonation lacked… flair.

"So," continues Moira, "you must be wondering why I'm here. I can hear the wheels in your brain spinning even at this distance."

As she moves on the walkway, a backpack slung over one shoulder swings beside her. Like her dress and the beret under which her hair is gathered, it is black. Add a lazily held Gauloise and she might pass for an aspiring French intellectual. Moira's words reflect her talent for mimicry; perhaps that now extends to fashion also.

Keep her talking. "Indeed," Arcadia says, "because it looks like you were enjoying your time in Paris."

Moira grins again. The stage lights make her face shine—is she sweating? But she is also pleased. "Oh *très bien*, Arky, *vachement bien*! You carry on demonstrating that you are more than just a bag of hammers. And when I heard that you were applying to Oxford, I thought to myself: Arky needs a memorable admissions test. Not the tedious interviews and written papers, but something that really does *test* you. Like the German philosopher with the whip says: that which does not kill us, makes us stronger. So I'd like to give you a test that really will make you stronger—because if you fail it, you die."

Something that is nearly fatal seems more likely to leave you weakened rather than strengthened—but it does not seem prudent to point that out to Moira right now.

"I can illustrate," the other her says, "with a story. Once upon a time, there was a teenage girl stranded on an island covered by forest. No Gilligan, no professor and Mary Ann, just the girl and her forest. On a day that a strong east wind is blowing, lightning strikes the easternmost point of the island and starts a fire. The flames devour everything in their path, fanned by the breeze and moving from east to west. The girl's island is two kilometres across; in two hours, the entire island will be consumed and the girl with it. The only beach is on the eastern tip and impossible to reach. The rest of the coast is cliffs or jagged rocks, so she cannot jump into the water, either."

Moira pauses for dramatic effect. "But the girl has read her Nietzsche and her will to live is strong. So how does she survive?"

"This is ridiculous," Henry says, pulling out his phone. "I'm calling the cops."

Arcadia puts her hand on his arm. "Wait a minute, Henry," she whispers. "I don't see any harm playing along with this game." With the door locked, there is also no escape other than past Moira.

Beside her, Dr. Bell shifts uneasily. Yet at the same time

he, too, seems intrigued by the problem. "I assume, young lady"—he clears his throat—"that our protagonist cannot call for help, and that there is no convenient stream to divert and thus extinguish the fire?"

Moira resumes pacing, one arm checking something in the backpack. "You assume correctly."

"What about a chainsaw?" Henry pipes up. "With a chainsaw she could cut a firebreak."

"There is no chainsaw," Moira replies. "Nor is there a fire hydrant, flame-resistant clothing, hydrogel, or a convenient hatch into a mysterious fireproof tunnel. Nothing. Just her wits."

Henry sniffs. "How has she been surviving on this island if she doesn't even have food and water?"

"Once again, Henry demonstrates all the intellectual sharpness of a mashed potato," says Moira, rolling her eyes. "Fine. She has all of that and a partridge in a pear tree—on the *eastern* side of the island. Now, can we get back to her imminent incineration?"

"She should start her own fire," Arcadia says quietly. "Use matches if she has them, or else take a branch to the edge of the current blaze and light it. Then run with it to the western side of the island. The wind will keep the new fire moving west, so if she can burn the trees on that side, once that fire is out she can shelter there when the original fire approaches."

"Oh bravo, Arky!" Moira seems genuinely pleased. "I am so glad I didn't kill you the last time we met. Normally, when I miss someone—which is rare—I take another shot and hit them the second time. But life without you would be like a broken pencil: pointless."

"This is all very interesting," says Henry, "but I suppose we should be getting on our way now. Nice seeing you, Moira, I guess. Thanks for not shooting me today."

"Please don't rush off, sweetie-pie," Moira calls. The forlorn tone in her voice hardens quickly: "Oh, that's right. You can't, because I've locked the door and have the only key. But you're right that this scene is dragging a little and so it's time to move on to our final game."

Moira points to the keypad next to the door. "You're familiar now with the good Dr. Bell's house of mirrors numerical system. Entertaining but a little— elementary, don't you think? I've edited the system that controls the lock so that you have one more task to complete." Again, the other her adjusts the backpack on her shoulder and then takes out a bottle.

"For this game," Moira continues, "we need three volunteers. Let's call them... Dr. Bell, Arky, and Henry. They are standing in a line and Dr. Bell is looking at Arky, but Arky is making cow eyes at Henry. As for Henry, he's staring blankly into space. Now, a key part of the game is that in this universe everyone is either guilty or innocent. Let's say—just for the purposes of argument—that Dr. Bell is guilty, but Henry is innocent. And your question is a simple one: is someone who is guilty looking at someone who is not?"

This is about more than just making admission to Oxford memorable. In her own peculiar way, Moira is trying to communicate something to her. But what? The bottle in her twin's hand is unlike the one she drank from when they last met. And it appears to have something sticking out of the top.

"Can I really not call the cops?" Henry whispers, a little too loudly. "She's obviously mad."

"'A madness most discreet,'" Moira replies. "'A choking gall, and a preserving sweet.'" Seeing his puzzled expression, the other her explains: "That was Shakespeare, Henry. *Romeo and Juliet*? You should read it one day. I was quoting Romeo and intimating that my outward appearance of mental disorganisation might be due to a romantic sentiment."

Henry's frown contradicts his nodding. "Oh, I see," he says, not seeing.

"Lighten up, Henry!" Moira replies, cheerily. "As they say: laughter is the best medicine." Then she frowns. "Actually, that's not entirely true. Not if you've got syphilis, for example. If you've got syphilis you're much better off with penicillin than with laughter." The other her pauses, train of thought apparently derailed. One hand holds the bottle with the cloth sticking out of the top, the other reaches into the bag and produces a cigarette lighter.

And then the flow of words resumes: "Anyhow, as I was saying, is a guilty person looking at an innocent person? You have one chance to answer and three choices: yes, no, or it's impossible to know. I suppose you do have a fourth option, which is not to tell me. But I'll just take that as the wrong answer and, well, you know how that goes."

The walls of the fake hotel room are wood and plasterboard. Difficult to smash through, but she and Henry might be able to use the furniture to climb out. Harder for Dr. Bell.

Moira has paused again, not due to confusion but in the manner of the host of a reality television programme. "So if your answer is 'yes', you press 1 on the keypad by the door. If it's 'no', you press 2. And if you decide it is impossible to know, you press 3. Correct answer opens the door. Anything else locks it and throws away the key." The other her regards the cigarette lighter. "Filthy habit, but the lighters are irresistible for those pyromaniacs among us." A practised flick of her thumb and a spark ignites the butane gas. An inch of flame now rises from her hand.

"I thought about giving you a time limit, but that's so been-there, done-that. Instead, I thought we could each estimate how long it will take for this pretend hotel room to burn to the ground. I'm afraid I don't think the fire marshals would be very impressed with this place, especially since the carpet has been doused with naphtha."

Moira now brings the lighter to the cloth sticking out of the bottle. It ignites immediately, probably soaked in alcohol or kerosene to serve as a wick. And when the bottle smashes, whatever is inside—petrol?—will spread the fire.

The other her lifts the bottle above her head, raising an eyebrow also. "Ready?"

"Oh no you don't." Beside her, Henry is preparing to do something rash. He still holds the phone with which he had planned to call the police, now being considered for one final missive.

"Henry," she begins, but his arm has already wound back and it is too late to stop him.

Thrown with force, the phone appears to travel a straight line towards Moira. Its true path would be a parabola with some adjustment for air resistance, but evolution and Henry's years of playing cricket mean that his aim is accurate even without using differential calculus. It hits the other her in the shoulder—was he aiming at her head?—knocking her sideways and causing her to drop the Molotov cocktail.

Henry's pleasure at hitting his target is evident, a small "Yes!" issuing from his lips. But the bottle falling from Moira's upstretched hand lands on the metal walkway and smashes. The liquid inside spreads across and through the platform, igniting a curtain of flame.

Standing in the middle of it, the other her stumbles as if confused. As she turns, her dress weaves in and out of the orange tongues. Fire needs oxygen, fuel, and heat. In seconds, the temperature of the cotton rises to the point that it, too, ignites. Tendrils of flame now rise up Moira's back as she raises her hands to cover her face. Surrounded by an aura of incandescence, she moves sideways but that only increases the oxygen supply, fanning the flames.

It is only seconds since the smash of the bottle, but the fire has made no sound. When the scream escapes Moira's lips it is more animal than human. More than pain, it is a cry of rage and frustration. This, surely, is not how Moira's final act was to play out: destroyed by her own weapon, dropped at her own feet. The other her cannot outrun the flames that trail her, yet now she races to the end of the elevated walkway. Stairs lead down to the ground beyond the mock hotel room but she cannot see. She stumbles. Hands still covering her face, she falls, disappearing behind the wall to land with a thud on the grass outside, wisps of smoke curling towards the marquee above.

"My God…" Henry begins, perhaps shocked at what he has done. But there will be time enough to deal with Moira's return and departure. For now, the fire from the walkway has engulfed the wall of the hotel room farthest from the door. And, true to her word, the carpet that would normally be fire-resistant has also ignited and a sheet of flame moves towards the three of them.

Smoke fills the room; even without a ceiling, soon there will not be enough oxygen to remain conscious. If it were possible to remove oxygen from the room completely, that would extinguish the fire—but also the lives of anyone inside. Nor is there any means of taking away the fuel or reducing the temperature. Flee, then.

Beside her, Dr. Bell is coughing but knows enough to back away from the flame and move towards the door.

Henry is motionless. It is a waste of oxygen, but she needs him to listen: "Henry," she calls. "Time to go."

He shakes his head as if to clear it and moves to the door also. On the walkway above them, his phone smoulders.

The door is locked and Moira said they only had one chance to open it. To do so, she has left them what is now her final problem. Dr. Bell is guilty and looking at Arky; Arky is looking at Henry, who is innocent.

"Oh crap," Henry says after a futile attempt to push the door open. "Moira and her bleeding puzzles. What did she want us to work out? Is a guilty person looking at an innocent one? You can't tell—we don't know whether this 'Arky' is guilty or innocent. So it's got to be number three."

He reaches for the button but this time she grabs his wrist. "Wait," she says firmly. There is more to this problem. "We don't know if she is guilty or innocent. But we do know that she is *either* guilty *or* innocent."

The heat is becoming as oppressive as the smoke and they now crouch near the door, Dr. Bell continuing to cough uncontrollably. Explanation can wait until later. But if the Arky in the problem must be either guilty or innocent, then even though it is impossible to know which she is, either she is innocent and being looked at by Dr. Bell, or she is guilty and she is looking at Henry.

Reaching up, she presses the mirrored symbol for "1" and there is a click as the magnetic lock releases. The door opens and they stumble outside, flames beginning to climb from the walls of the stage to the marquee above. Dr. Bell is struggling to stand, so she and Henry take one arm each and pull him out onto the lawn. Fresh air fills their lungs and they collapse onto the grass, noticing for the first time the cries of a gathering crowd and the peal of a fire alarm.

She turns to watch as the marquee burns, an acrid smell filling the air. The plastic of the tent must have been treated also, accelerating the conflagration. Then the aluminium frame begins to buckle and the marquee collapses in on itself like a marshmallow left to roast too long, a funeral pyre for the twin sister she never got to know.

2
LOST

It is late afternoon when she reaches Mother, just before dinner is served at the small hospital near the Priory School. Nurses and orderlies give her a familiar smile, but there is pity in their eyes as they carry on their business or simply look away.

After passing the one-year mark, the chances of Mother waking from her coma have moved from slim to all but non-existent. In their gentle way Aunt Jean and Uncle Arthur, her guardians since the attack on her parents, have begun suggesting that Louisa—Mother—might not have wanted to live like this for months, for years.

Rationally, she knows this. Rationally, there is no basis for expecting any change, any improvement. Though there are stories of miraculous awakenings after a decade or more, these fairy tales tend not to dwell on the quality of life after recovery. Rationally, Mother is already dead.

And yet. Standing beside Mother; holding her hand,

warm but limp. She cannot simply look at this through actuarial tables of survival and recovery. Mother was reduced to this state by her former Headmaster. Milton killed Father on the same night, part of a crazed plan to move Arcadia from their care to his, the better to develop her intellectual powers. None of this would have happened had she not tugged at the web of lies enveloping her school. At the time, she thought she was at the centre of an experiment—a laboratory rat being observed and prodded. Milton admitted that much, before he was killed by Miss Alderman. The substitute teacher had inveigled herself into the Priory School to observe her, but ended up saving her life. Later, Miss Alderman had asked Arcadia to forgive her, but could not bring herself to say for what.

All that changed when she met Moira. A twin but more than a twin, Moira's genes were manipulated to enhance her intelligence. Arcadia might be bright, but Moira is— was incandescent. Before Lysander Starr was killed in the explosion, Arcadia learned that she was not at the centre of an experiment but merely the control—an expendable placebo. *Moira* was the true test subject, the rat that escaped its lab. And now she is gone.

Normally, Arcadia introduces herself to Mother when she visits. She might talk about the weather, about school. Today she simply takes out her violin and plays.

After the fire, as the flames of the burning marquee died down, police came to take their statements. She watched two paramedics carry a stretcher from the smouldering remains, a blanket covering the body from head to toe. As they stepped from the lawn onto the paving stones, a black sleeve flopped over the edge of the stretcher, a charred hand dangling as if it were waving. She looked away.

There was no point dissembling now, so she told the local police officer all. Or most of it. That she had an estranged, unstable, twin sister who had tried to kill her. Although even that wasn't quite true—once again, Moira had given her a test and she had passed. The consequences of failing would have been severe, but what were to be the consequences of succeeding? She explained to the officer that she had been adopted and did not know the full circumstances of her sister's upbringing, that they met only once before. Why had she not reported that at the time, the officer asked.

Why indeed? At the time she thought she might be able to find out more without interference. But a year ago Moira and Miss Alderman both vanished, even as Starr's death removed her closest connection to the experiment. Magnus tried to help track down more information but the trail went cold. And, she has to admit, learning that she was the control in an experiment—rather than its focus—diminished the urgency of her search. Milton's attack on her parents was not part of a grand conspiracy, as neither he nor Miss Alderman knew of Moira's existence. It was a tragedy, but a meaningless one.

To the police officer, all she said was that it had been a shock to discover she had a sister and that no harm had actually been done beyond the fire. She did not link

Moira to the death of Lysander Starr—or mention the unfortunate Mr. Pratt, another teacher whose death had been classified as a suicide. The officer noted all this down, took her contact details, promised to be in touch. As the attacker in this incident had died, there would be inquiries into her identity and the circumstances of her death—but further action by the police was unlikely.

Dr. Bell was profuse in his apologies as she and Henry walked back to the Porter's Lodge to collect their luggage for their return journey to the Priory School. "I'm so relieved that no harm came to you," he said, still shaken by the episode. "Indeed, it is I who owe you a debt of gratitude for saving my life on a second occasion."

"It's hard to believe that Moira is gone," Arcadia replied.

On reflection, it is almost impossible to believe. Moira's capacity to plan, to take contingencies into account—how could she die in such a banal way: by dropping the weapon that consumed her?

"What did Moira mean when she said 'It's always apples'?" she asked as they arrived at the Lodge.

"I haven't the foggiest idea," Dr. Bell mused. "I never met the girl before. I'm discounting, of course, the occasion when she drugged me and I woke up with a bomb strapped to my chest. Perhaps on that occasion there happened to be an apple on my desk?"

Perhaps. It was hardly the strangest thing Moira had said or done. Dr. Bell bade them farewell and she and Henry departed the college walls to wait for the bus.

The music leaves her bow, vibrating strings of the violin coming to rest with the final note. In the small room there is a slight echo, molecules of air carrying the memory of the tune until they, too, return to an equilibrium of random motion and silence.

She places the instrument back in its case and takes out one of Mother's diaries. She has read all three journals now, each begun at a turning point in Mother's life. The first recounts her courtship and marriage to Father. The second covers Magnus's birth and early years. The final volume, the one that Moira sent her after stealing all three, focuses on her own birth and development. The entries are not daily; sometimes months go by with only a word. But it is a window into Mother's past, and the only way in which her voice reaches the present.

Occasionally she reads aloud from the diaries, choosing a page randomly. Though she and Mother share no genetic bond, years of conversation mean that she hears echoes of Mother even as the words leave her own mouth. Nature and nurture once again. Today she flips to the last pages that Mother wrote in the third diary, the volume that tracks her own life from birth to this final vignette:

3 January 2007—I can't believe Arky turns seven on Saturday. Magnus says it feels more like seventy

years, but he's just grouchy because Arky chose
carrot cake over chocolate.

She finally told me today what she wanted for
her birthday: a diamond! How simply delightful, I
thought. My baby girl is starting to get interested
in princesses and jewellery at last. Then Ignatius
told me it was for something called a Mohs scale.
Apparently it measures how hard things are on a
scale of one to ten by seeing if one of them can
scratch the others. She's got her hands on nine
stones from talc to topaz and this will complete the
set. Ignatius thinks he can get an industrial diamond
that won't break the bank. And there I was about to
go shopping for earrings.

She pauses and takes Mother's hand. "I'm sorry I was
never a very 'girly' girl," she says. "But I did love the
diamond you and Father got me. And I still have the Mohs
scale—though topaz is only number eight."

She keeps reading:

For the umpteenth time, I told Arky the story
about the blind old woman and the bird. I think she
understands it now, but I'm not entirely sure if that
means that she gets it in her heart as well as in her
head. I hope she does.

Come Saturday we'll draw another line on the doorframe. I'm resigned to Arky never being tall—it's like her body puts all of her energy into that brain of hers. But she's strong, stronger than Magnus even. (I've long given up trying to persuade that boy to stop treating his body like an amusement park, as Mrs Costanza might say.)

Each morning Arky and I now do sit-ups and push-ups together, along with a bit of yoga. It's our mother-daughter time while the menfolk doze. And three times a week we go swimming. All part of giving her a healthy mind in a healthy body—"mens sana in corpore sano"—just like the professor told me to.

And the diary ends. She tries not to let it show in her voice, but the final words shock her, as they always do. How much of Mother's relationship with her was genuine, and how much was scripted? This is the only mention the diary makes of a professor; elsewhere it is "he" or "they".

She flicks through the remaining blank pages. The only markings are a doodle on the inside back cover of the journal. Even Mother's doodles are precise, however, and the stylised drawing of a tree has carefully positioned dots to show its ripe fruit.

No explanation is given for ending the diary at that point, but after recording seven years of Magnus's life,

Mother's sense of fairness might have compelled her to document at least the same amount of her own. Then perhaps she put the journal aside and simply failed to pick it up again. Or maybe she was told to stop?

Her reverie is interrupted by a presence at the doorway behind her. Its actual effect on the air pressure in the room must be so small as to be unmeasurable, yet she can sense the mass of her brother. "Well look what we have here," she says to Mother. "If it isn't my mother's son. How nice to see you, Magnus." She turns as he enters the room, gravitating towards the sturdier of two chairs on the other side of the bed. His tailored shirt, expensive and expansive, has been hastily brushed for crumbs, though a streak of red is visible. "Still treating dessert as an appetiser, I see. Jam doughnut?"

"Raspberry tart," he corrects her testily, removing his coat and sitting down. "Everything in moderation, Arcadia—including moderation. It's nice to see you too. Your interviews at Oxford appear to have gone well." He sniffs. "Did you visit a plastics factory on the way back? Oh, and hello, Mother," he adds, patting her hand.

"Off work early, today?" she inquires. "This new job of yours doesn't seem to be particularly taxing."

"As it happens," Magnus begins, "I am here on business. I knew you were likely to come down this evening and thought I might catch up with you and see Mother at the same time."

"What sort of 'business'?"

Magnus looks to the ground and then at her. "As

astonishing as this may seem," he says, "I am in need of your help. A certain matter has come across my desk and you have a unique connection to the problem and, we hope, the solution."

"Who, exactly, is 'we'?"

He ignores the question. "It seems that your little friend has been stealing."

"My little friend—do you mean Moira?" Prior to the confrontation with her twin sister a year earlier, Moira had tricked Magnus into revealing information about her. It was a rare occurrence and still clearly smarted.

"Yes," he replies curtly. "Your doppelgänger has engaged in an act of burglary that, while impressive as a matter of craft, has the potential to be embarrassing to some individuals of the highest—"

"She died today, Magnus," Arcadia says quietly.

He pauses, forehead creasing into a frown. "I beg your pardon?"

"Moira died today," she repeats.

"Yes, well that's rather unlikely, don't you think?" he replies. "As I was saying, the theft—"

"I saw it myself. She was on fire." There is some evidence that the memory of an event stimulates the same parts of the brain activated during the event itself. As the image of Moira on fire comes back to her, she almost smells the acrid smoke once more.

Magnus sighs. "What, exactly, did you see?"

She describes the escape room and the tests, Moira's

appearance holding a bottle with petrol or some other flammable liquid. Henry hitting her with his phone.

"His phone?" Magnus shakes his head. "I would have thought a shoe would do the trick. Carry on."

The bottle smashing at her feet. Her standing in the flames.

"And then?"

"And then her entire body was on fire," Arcadia says, closing her eyes.

"Really?" Magnus presses. "That seems somewhat hard to believe. Skin is almost two-thirds water and quite difficult to ignite. There is much less water in hair, so it will burn at a significantly lower temperature."

The beret. "Her hair—" Arcadia begins. "Her hair was covered by a beret. But her clothes, her clothes were burning. There's no way she could have survived."

"So what you're saying is that her pants were on fire?" Magnus is enjoying this a little too much.

"It was a dress. But she screamed. And fell. I heard the sound of her body hitting the ground." Even as she recounts it to Magnus, she begins to see the holes. "The paramedics carried her out on a stretcher," she murmurs, almost to herself. "Or two people dressed as paramedics carried someone out on a stretcher. The face was covered."

"I see," Magnus says. "Come, Arcadia, put yourself in the position of the person you are trying to understand. Climb into her skin and walk around in it, just like Mother taught us."

Mother? Vague memories of childhood games surface, role-playing characters but also reliving moments. Mother pressing her to see a grievance through the other person's eyes. And Moira saying something similar—quoting, of course—at their first meeting.

If memory is, to the brain, indistinguishable from the event itself, then why should imagining an event be any different? She closes her eyes and experiences it as Moira might have. Past events once lay in the future, and can be recreated in the present.

I hold the bottle of fire above me as a provocation, as a target. I have prepared for this: black clothes covering my body, hair tucked into a beret, face shiny not with sweat but with—fire-retardant gel.

Predictably, it is Henry who takes the bait; sacrificing his phone even as Arky tries to stop him. Pain shoots through my shoulder but it makes the acting easier. I release the bottle and allow it to drop onto the metal walkway, bottom first. The thin glass smashes upon impact, spreading its hydrocarbon contents across the metal walkway even as the wick follows, bringing flame to the fuel.

Now time for my conflagration, it begins as a flicker.

Light dances with the shadows, moving as I move. There is no sound, no crackling. No smoke.

I turn in slow motion, a duet with the orange tongues that now lap at my dress. Stop, drop, and roll? I am— I appear disoriented. Wandering this way and that, I only fan the tendrils that now climb up my back.

Hands over my face. Protecting it from heat but only delaying the inevitable. Still I move, unable to escape the incandescence that trails me like an aura. It is terrible; it is beautiful.

Until at last a primal scream erupts from my lips as the flames engulf me. The pain is real, but I run and the heat trails behind. I reach the end of the walkway and jump. The thud as I land is also real, but the foam I land in extinguishes the fire, starving it of oxygen and leeching out the heat.

I prepare for my exit but this crime scene needs a body. It is impractical to play that role myself; eventually I would need to revive. And so I plant a twin. Or a triplet?

"Why would she go through this?" Arcadia asks, opening her eyes.

"To disappear?" The uncertainty in Magnus's voice is uncharacteristic.

"But she *had* disappeared. She vanished for a year."

"From you, perhaps," Magnus says. "But maybe you were not the person she needed to convince."

And so the other her lit a fire in order to hide in its ashes.

"Very well," Arcadia concedes. "It is possible that she is still alive. So what is it that you believe she stole?"

Magnus stands and moves towards the window in Mother's room. "An item of jewellery and some animals," he says, turning to face her.

The precise scope of Magnus's job remains unclear, but chasing down burglars and cattle rustlers would be an odd use of his time—and unlikely to be something to which he would apply the slightest effort. Yet this matter came across his desk. Not just any jewellery, then. Some very special jewellery.

"There have been no reports of any theft from the Tower," she says.

"When it comes to the preservation of the Crown itself, we deem it appropriate for the press to operate on a need-to-know basis. At present they and the general public do not need to know."

"Why do you think it was Moira who stole this jewellery? Was she seen, were there witnesses?"

"No." Magnus strokes his chin, looking out the window. "As I said, as a matter of craft this was a perfectly executed burglary. The security systems were disabled; the guards incapacitated. Only one very specific jewel was taken—St. Edward's Sapphire. I had previously been of assistance in locating the sapphire when it was stolen a little more than a year ago while on display at a local museum. On that occasion, a private collector commissioned its theft."

"By Moira?"

"I now believe so." Magnus nods. "This may have been how she financed her existence, through operating as a kind of consultant on criminal matters. Or maybe she was bored. Or it was practice."

"If she is so clever, how is it that she left a trail of evidence leading to her?"

"She did not leave evidence," Magnus counters. "She left a note. Or, to be precise, she left *you* a note. It was inside the bullet-proof glass casing this morning, surrounded by motion sensors. When the system came back online, in place of a priceless, thousand-year-old gemstone was a letter addressed to you. This letter."

He reaches into his jacket pocket and produces a folded sheet of paper. "There were some suggestions," he continues, "that you should be brought in for questioning. But I managed to persuade the relevant authorities that it was best if I handled this quietly."

"You're working with the Home Office now?"

"In a manner of speaking." He hands her the piece of off-white bond paper on which is printed, in a familiar elegant font:

Why is a raven like a writing desk?

Not much of a letter. "I assume you've tested it for fingerprints and the like," she says, holding it up to the light to check for invisible ink.

"Naturally," Magnus intones. "There are no foreign bodies whatsoever. She appears to have handled the note wearing surgical gloves in a cleanroom. Most impressive."

The riddle itself is, of course, familiar. A Mad Hatter's Tea-Party. Would that make her Alice in Wonderland, with Moira as the Mad Hatter? Aloud, she says: "Why ask a famously unanswerable riddle? There's no correct response—or there are many. They both have inky quills. One is a pest for wrens; the other is a rest for pens. Lewis Carroll got so sick of people demanding a correct answer that thirty years later he provided one that was as good— or as bad—as any other: they both produce notes."

She turns the paper over in her hands. "I do appreciate the irony, though, of leaving it at the Tower of London."

"You recall, then, the Legend of the Ravens?"

Years ago, they visited the Tower as a family. Magnus, a staunch monarchist even as a teenager, had insisted that they budget an entire day for the visit and came with questions that flummoxed even the most patient tour guides. She would have been seven at the time. When they saw the eight ravens then living at the Tower, she recalls feeling troubled by the fact that their wings had been clipped to prevent escape. The legend provides a reason, if not a justification: "'If the Tower of London ravens are lost or fly away,'" she quotes, "'the Crown will fall and Britain with it.'"

"Precisely," Magnus says. Waiting.

She knows that he is fishing for something. Pausing for her to catch up with him. As always, it is infuriating and enticing. Something more about ravens. "You said she stole some animals. The ravens?"

"*All* the ravens," Magnus lowers his voice. "As you can imagine, both matters are a cause of some concern.

Within the hour we deployed the reserve ravens held in a nearby aviary. These will fool most casual observers. But some members of the public are quite—dedicated, shall we say?—when it comes to our Royal Family. There are those outside the Tower who know the individual birds by sight. And as for those within the Tower, one can only keep a secret for so long. Hence my journey here to solicit your assistance in locating jewel and birds."

"What would Moira want with the ravens?"

"Motive is a useful analytical lens, but I am primarily concerned not with *why* she did it than with *how* to recover that which has been taken. Similarly, I hope you will agree to assist in this matter out of civic virtue. But if you need more encouragement, then I suggest you look more closely at the note that Moira left for you."

She examines the letter once more. Laser printed characters in a familiar font. No invisible ink, not even fingerprints on the off-white bond paper. What led Magnus to say that it was addressed to her?

And then she sees it. The same paper with two lines of dancing men. Another sheet bearing a code within a code. And an envelope of the same paper with an "A" written in Mother's flourished handwriting, steak knife fixing it to the corkboard.

"This is the same paper that Mother used for our codes at home," she whispers. On Saturdays, for as long as she could remember, Mother would set her a puzzle to solve. That stopped with the attack, at which time she discovered that it was not Mother setting the codes but the former Headmaster, Milton.

Moira has written to her before, with the same script but on ordinary paper. Now the other her has contrived to use the same paper that Milton used. But what message is being communicated? And how does Magnus think she can help find the missing jewel?

Unless he doesn't. And unless there is no message.

"You don't want me to find the sapphire," she says at last. "You just think that I can lead you to Moira. You didn't come here to ask for my help—you want to use me as bait."

Magnus has suddenly become concerned about Mother's comfort and is reshaping the pillow under her head. Confirmation that her suspicions are correct.

"But if Moira stole the jewel last night and faked her own death today, what makes you think that she will turn up here?"

"Moira does seem to have something of a fascination with you," Magnus observes, smoothing the sheets to remove some of the creases.

"And something of a knack for manipulating you," she counters. Light a fire and then hide in the ashes. "Has it occurred to you that this note might not be intended for me but for you? It's a perfect storm to ensure that it captured your attention: mystery, family, and royalty. You may be brilliant, Magnus, but you are also predictable."

Her brother's face is never easy to read and the clenching of a jaw muscle is the only indication of tension, but his voice remains even. "Of course I considered that possibility, but—"

He pauses as his phone rings, a choral rendition of "Rule, Britannia". A glance at the caller and he puts the phone to his ear. "Yes?"

As he listens, the flexing of the muscle in his jaw causes the skin at his temple to ripple. He takes a few steps as if to leave, but decides that his sister and unconscious mother pose less of a risk than unknown parties outside. He closes the door.

"I did nothing of the sort," he protests, temple almost vibrating as he listens to the other end of the line. "I'm on my way back now. In the meantime please execute a shutdown of my system until I come in for biometric verification." Another pause. "What do you mean you have biometric verification? An iris scan? Obviously I am *not* onsite or we wouldn't be having this conversation. I knew it was a mistake going out into the field."

He picks up his coat and prepares to leave, but continues to listen. "'Thank you'? Thank you for what?" he says, switching hands to put his coat on. His face is beginning to redden—capillaries dilating with embarrassment, stress, or just the exertion of moving faster than usual. Then for the first time he raises his voice: "Oh for the love of— What possesses you to think that I would order pizza for everyone in the building?" His eyes go to the ceiling as the caller replies. "Hmm," he grunts, calming somewhat. "Pepperoni, you say? Oh very well. Tell them I shall post them a cheque. But I want a twelve-inch put aside for me."

He hangs up and drops the phone in his pocket. Turning back to face her he opens his mouth and then closes it again.

"You have to go?" she offers.

"Yes."

"Can you at least tell me what you think Moira might have been looking for in your system?"

He hesitates—protecting his pride, national security, or the air of mystery he now cultivates? "I have been entrusted with certain contracts for our Ministry of Defence. If these fell into the wrong hands it would be…" A frown crosses his brow and then subsides as he settles on the appropriate word: "Delicate."

"And you now suspect that Moira would be after this for what, money?"

"Money and power motivate people to do all manner of strange things. Not all of us are driven by the satisfaction of our appetites; some want even more than that." He notices for the first time the jam stain on his shirt, picking some of the raspberry off and raising it thoughtfully to his lips. "Anyway, I had best be off."

He kisses Mother on the forehead and extends his left hand to Arcadia. It is a touching gesture and she allows him to hold her own, at which point he produces a ballpoint pen and prepares to write. "May I?"

The similarity to cattle-branding is galling, but a

physical distinction between herself and Moira could be useful. She rolls up her sleeve so that he can mark her arm with his looping signature.

"A temporary measure at best," he concedes, "but I would prefer to avoid being fooled by Moira again."

"Tell me, Magnus," she asks, pulling her sleeve back down as he reopens the door, "which part of the government do you work for?"

"All of it, my dear Arcadia. All of it." And with his best Cheshire Cat grin he turns on his heel and is gone.

3
FOUND

"Good morning, ladies and gentlemen," Mr. Ormiston says, raising his hands for quiet. From the lectern he surveys students and staff as whispered conversations die down to silence. A nod to the organist and they stand:

God save our gracious Queen!
Long live our noble Queen...

The final days of Michaelmas Term see the student body thin, some parents choosing family holidays over the busywork of post-exam school. She plans to stay on until the end, before heading to Aunt Jean and Uncle Arthur's farm for Christmas. Magnus will likely join them—though given the temper in which he departed the hospital yesterday, it is not clear he will be in a mood to celebrate.

Long to reign over us:
God save the Queen!

The shuffling of several hundred students preparing to sit is interrupted by the peals of the organ introducing the second verse of the national anthem, normally reserved for special occasions like graduation. They straighten and sing:

Thy choicest gifts in store
On her be pleased to pour,
Long may she reign.

Calls for preservation of the monarch and a long reign reflect a desire for political stability, but is it really necessary to ask the deity to shower yet more material wealth upon the woman? Or perhaps it is an injunction against commoners presuming to desire that wealth for themselves. Or steal it from the Tower.

May she defend our laws,
And ever give us cause,
To sing with heart and voice,
God save the Queen!

A moment of uncertainty follows the organ's last chord, until Mr. Ormiston impatiently gestures for the students to be seated. "We are entering the final days of term," he says, "and of a calendar year that has been a happily uneventful one."

There is some hesitant laughter. The previous year saw the deaths of a headmaster and two teachers—the former by defenestration, the latter by suicide and when a car was blown up with military-grade explosives on the school grounds. Mr. Ormiston took on the role as acting Headmaster in these uncertain circumstances, before being appointed formally in September at the start of the current academic year.

"Now that your exams are finished," Mr. Ormiston continues, "and those of you going for Oxbridge interviews have completed them, I thought we might do something a little different at the Priory School before term ends next week." One of the teachers coughs, causing Mr. Ormiston to turn as if inviting a comment. There is none. "We have long functioned under the Code of Conduct, with a clear hierarchy from teachers to Headmaster to implement it. Students who perform well are praised and rewarded; students who misbehave may be sanctioned—put off grub, given a detention, or in extreme cases rusticated."

Being put "off grub" is a quaint term for being denied desserts and other treats. Detention usually means spending time at or near Headmaster's office. Rustication is the euphemism for being sent home, though literally it means being sent to the countryside—more suggestive of China's Cultural Revolution than public school discipline.

"We do not, of course, condone corporal punishment

at the Priory School." Mr. Ormiston coughs, catching her eye briefly. As they both know, the late Mr. Pratt was one of those who practised—relished, even—physically disciplining the youth in his care. "Nevertheless, many assume that your good behaviour is driven by fear of punishment rather than the inherent virtue of our young men and women.

"As yearlings"—he refers to first-year students at the Priory School—"you each read William Golding's *Lord of the Flies*. Many assume that, left to their own devices, children will swiftly descend into savagery." He pauses to cast his eyes across the seated students. "I, for one, have a more optimistic view of human nature. With that in mind, we are suspending the Code for the remainder of term and your teachers will be refraining from interfering in any matter that does not threaten lasting injury or property damage. Classes will continue, but your reports have already been written and there will be no school punishment for failing to attend."

A free market approach to discipline? Or free range? The prospect of no punishments causes a flutter of conversation, which Mr. Ormiston does not raise a hand to silence. After waiting for it to fade, he explains that there are responsibilities as well as rights in this new system: "I am also giving a holiday to our service staff. Many of you take these men and women for granted; for the coming week you will be doing their jobs. It is up to you how that is organised. The cooks will remain on duty for today's lunch, but after that you are to prepare meals yourselves. Serving and cleaning up after meals will also be up to you, as will be keeping the grounds and buildings clean."

He finishes speaking and steps back from the lectern. Among the teaching staff, seated in chairs on one side of the raised platform, some eyebrows are raised. Among the students, the murmur is now punctuated by a couple of cheers. As Mr. Ormiston, Headmaster now in name only, does not return to the lectern, it gradually dawns on the students that they are free to leave. They do so uncertainly, some wondering whether it is appropriate to exit before being dismissed, others suspecting that the lifting of punishments is a trick.

She remains in her seat, watching the teaching staff. From their body language this is not a surprise—but not all are convinced that it is a good idea.

A mop of blond hair flops down next to her. "So," Henry says, "how do you think the inmates will do running the asylum?"

"Hmm," she replies absently. Mr. Ormiston is a dedicated teacher, passionate about the school and its students. Is he really testing his faith in their virtue?

"Have you heard anything more from the Oxford police?" Henry asks. "Do they have any more information about where Moira came from, or what the crazy bird was up to?"

"No," she says. "I'm still trying to work out how she did it."

"Did what?"

"The body they carried out. The fire I can see: once her clothes were extinguished she escaped out of the back of the tent. But whose body did they carry out? Even though it was burned to a crisp, Moira must know that they are going to try to identify it. So who was it?"

"You think she's *alive*?" Henry's voice rises. At the front of Hall the music teacher, Mrs. Norman-Neruda, raises her head to tell him to be quiet before stopping herself. He lowers his tone nonetheless: "Why come back after a year only to light yourself up like a candle? It doesn't make any sense. Not that your twin has really established herself as a person who cares about making sense."

"I don't know—yet. With Moira there's always some kind of plan. But she's like a Rube Goldberg machine."

"A what?" Henry runs a hand through his hair. "Oh, you mean those things where a candle burns through a rope that releases a bowling ball that knocks over a block of wood that catapults a rubber duck into a basket in order to switch on a light?"

"Er, yes," she says. "Something that completes a task in the most complicated manner possible. Moira seems less interested in the end, whatever her goal is, than the means." Losing the other her completely—and then realising that her twin was still alive—has given rise to a curious feeling that goes beyond the satisfaction of an elegant solution. Warmth? Something more than just another problem to solve.

Henry is looking at her strangely. "You're starting to *like* her?"

She ponders this. "Let's just say that I'm glad she's not dead."

"Yet," Henry adds, shaking his head. "Anyway, are you going to class? I gather that's now optional."

"In a minute," she replies. From the front of Hall she sees Mr. Ormiston walking towards them. "I just need to speak to Mr. Ormiston. I'll see you there."

Henry heads off, nodding to Mr. Ormiston as he does.

"Good morning, Miss Greentree," Headmaster says. "I heard about the fire at Oxford. And something concerning a twin?"

Does he know that Moira visited the Priory School a year ago, that she took Arcadia's place? Did he meet her? He will find out soon enough, but with the knowledge that Moira is still alive she is economical with the truth.

"Yes," she says. "It was shocking to me, too."

Seeing that she will volunteer nothing more, he sighs. "Arcadia, you know that there are people around you who want to help. To discover that you have a sibling—a twin that you'd never met—is a pretty big event. I'm sorry that you didn't feel you could share that with me."

He is disappointed, but in her or in himself? He continues to be a difficult person to read. Trustworthy but not reliable, she once concluded. Perhaps that is what he is testing now in his students, whether he can rely on them?

"I had best get to class," she says. "Even without the

threat of detention, my Aunt and Uncle are still paying fees."

She is on a half-scholarship but he does not correct her. "Very well, Arcadia. You know where to find me if you want to talk. In the meantime, please look after our more vulnerable pupils. I do have confidence in our students, but what we are doing over the next week carries some risks. Keep an eye out?"

"Don't I always?" she replies, turning to follow the unruly mass leaving Hall.

It is around lunchtime that the first cracks in the new regime begin to emerge. Solidarity among students gives way to the need for order.

The focus of the dispute is the midday meal and who should serve it. The chefs are preparing cutlets and vegetables, but serving trays have not been laid out and there are no dishes or cutlery. A queue of hungry teenagers has begun to form, while one or two have gone straight into the kitchen to take a piece of lamb with their hands to eat on the quadrangle.

Surprisingly, it is Sebastian Harker who steps up with an apparently altruistic proposal. In the past, Sebastian was engaged by the former Headmaster as part of "provocation protocols" to see how Arcadia responded to stress. Magnus once said that similar tests were used to evaluate government agents for fieldwork. Since Milton's passing, Sebastian has reverted to being merely annoying.

He is almost a head taller than most of the students and able to project his voice so that all can hear him. "All right guys," he says to the crowd gathering outside Hall. "We need a system here. Upper sixth will serve this meal, lower sixth will clean up. Fifth form will serve dinner and remove"—the school's term for second-year students—"will clear. Yearlings are on grounds duty today. Upper sixes, you're with me, OK?" Without waiting for an answer, he heads into the kitchen. After a moment's hesitation, the upper sixth students follow. At his side, Joan Hardy whispers into his ear. "Oh right," he says, turning back to the group. "Wash hands first, everyone."

Taking on the first set of duties is uncharacteristic of the Sebastian she has come to know. Is it possible that he has matured over the years at the Priory School? Possible. But as she joins the group preparing cutlery for the students—their teachers, it seems, have decided to pack lunches rather than watch their charges struggle through the first meal alone—she sees Sebastian and Joan exchange knowing looks. Neither has much potential as a poker player: it is evident that they are planning something.

Precisely what it is remains unclear through the course of the meal. After the others have started their lunch, the upper sixth students take their food also and sit down. Sebastian ostentatiously insists on taking his food last, not even complaining when there are no more chips and he is forced to settle for mashed potato.

By starting the roster he has established a kind of authority. But is he also taking the biblical notion that the last shall be first literally? In any case, he is not one to delay gratification—no second marshmallow for him—and it will not be long before his intentions become clearer.

She, on the other hand, is prepared to wait and to watch. Henry sits opposite her, gnawing absent-mindedly on a bone.

Towards the end of the meal, the lower sixth form students begin the unfamiliar task of clearing dishes. With what he thinks is a subtle wink at Joan, Sebastian extends his leg as part of an exaggerated yawn, tripping one of the lower sixes—a harmless boy by the name of Arthur Saltire—as he passes while carrying the remains of six dishes of pudding.

Boy, crockery, and pudding tumble to the ground with a crash. Arthur is uninjured, though he lies in a shallow pool of dessert. But Sebastian's trouser leg has also caught a fleck of custard and he stands up in outrage. "You did that on purpose!" he declares.

Bewildered, Arthur looks up at the larger boy and mouths that it was an accident. He played a decent Hamlet in last year's student performance, but now looks genuinely frightened.

"An accident?" Sebastian mocks his voice, looking around for support or at least for an audience. "I think you resented having to clean up. You didn't like doing some honest, decent work, and so you were careless. You sauntered down the aisle without a care for who or what you might bump into."

"No, I really didn't—"

"Don't interrupt!" Sebastian shouts. He regards the other students, daring anyone to intervene on behalf of the miscreant.

Opposite her, Henry begins to stand but she puts a hand on his forearm to stop him. Sebastian is looking for a confrontation; there is little value in giving one to him.

"Listen," Sebastian says, his voice oozing with reasonableness. "I'm prepared to give you the benefit of the doubt. But we're going to need some kind of order around here, now that the teachers are skiving off. So I shall be keeping a book. Consider this your yellow card. But remember that another yellow card means you get a red card. And you *don't* want to get a red card."

Are the ethics of football to govern the school, then? From his pocket, Sebastian produces a small notebook and asks Arthur for his name. Writing carefully in the book, he puts it back in his pocket and stretches out his leg once more for Arthur to clean the custard off with a napkin. He then stands and leaves Hall, Joan hurrying along beside him.

As they pass her, she hears Joan whisper: "What happens when they get a red card?"

Sebastian's reply comes with a smirk: "Wait and see."

"Miss Greentree?" At the entrance to Hall Mr. McMurdo looks anxious. Something or someone unexpected has arrived and the school porter has been thrown off his schedule.

She and Henry have almost finished helping Arthur clean up from his tumble, broken crockery piled onto a tray. He will need to change clothes before going back to class in the afternoon—though of course that is now optional.

"Go on," Henry says. "We'll be fine. Right, Arthur?"

The younger boy gives a half-hearted upturning of the lips and she heads out to see what has discombobulated Mr. McMurdo.

"Good afternoon, Mr. McMurdo," she says. "How is everything?"

The porter frowns. "Well, I don't mind tellin' ye that I ain't comfortable with this no-rules lark. 'Jus' make sure the children ain't at each other's throats', they tell me." He shakes his head. "There's a natural order to things that needs keepin'. Anyhow, you have visitors, you do. Come to the lodge just now askin' to see you."

A family member would have telephoned. A random visitor would have been turned away. Someone with authority but wanting to follow procedures scrupulously.

"Is it the police?" she asks as they head across the quadrangle to the lodge.

Mr. McMurdo looks at her, vacillating between suspicion and concern. "Aye, missy." He hesitates, before adding: "'Taint none of my concern, but were you expectin' them?"

"No," she replies. "But perhaps I should have been."

They enter the lodge and the two officers stand. "Inspector Bradstreet, Constable Lestrange, what an unexpected pleasure," she says warmly. "You should have telephoned."

School policy is—or was—that phones are to be switched off during the day. She has taken to leaving hers on silent mode, but there were no calls. Lestrange, at least, has her telephone number. Are they following procedure, or did they not want to warn her of their arrival?

"Good afternoon, Miss Greentree," Constable Lestrange says. "It's been a while."

Inspector Bradstreet is in no mood for pleasantries. "A twin, Miss Greentree? You have a twin? I suppose you merely forgot to mention that when we were investigating the death of Mr. Pratt. Suddenly your alibi at the time he died doesn't look quite so sound, does it?"

She looks shocked, or does her best to look shocked: "I was as surprised as anyone to find out." Now she furrows her brow with confusion. "But I thought that Mr. Pratt was found to have committed suicide. And didn't his wife plead guilty to perverting the course of justice?"

"Don't play dumb with me, Miss Greentree," Inspector Bradstreet glowers. "You really think you're the cheese that makes the moon, don't you?"

"Er, I'm not sure that's a thing, sir," Lestrange interjects.

"Shut up, Constable," Bradstreet fumes at him, before turning back to her. "You may have the schoolmasters here convinced by your halo-polishing routine, Miss Greentree, but I know better."

Mr. McMurdo has been sorting mail but now he looks up. "Is everything all right, Miss Greentree?" the porter inquires.

"Yes, thanks," she says. Turning back to the visitors, she asks: "As I told your counterparts in Oxford, I knew virtually nothing about Moira. I didn't even know I was adopted until the week my parents were attacked." She contemplates dabbing her eyes, but too quick a succession of emotions will come across as insincere. "Let alone that I had a twin. Have they learned anything from the body?"

It is Constable Lestrange who replies. "Not much— it was burned beyond recognition. From what we do have, she's a complete Jane Doe. There's no record of her anywhere in our systems. It's like she didn't exist."

Inspector Bradstreet snorts as if this happens regularly. "You're just lucky that she's got unique fingerprints, which should enable us to establish that it's not actually you that's dead." He pauses, realising what he has just said. "I bet you didn't know that even identical twins have different fingerprints, did you?"

She does, but knows it would be unproductive to say as much. Confining herself to an exaggerated "Oh", she waits for him to say what he has come to say.

"In any case," Bradstreet presses on, reverting to television caricature, "we are not here on a social call. We received a tip-off and would like to request that you let us search your room. We don't yet have a warrant, but we can get one. When I explained this to your Headmaster, he said that with your permission we could clear this all up quite quickly."

Search her room for what? There is nothing to connect her to Mr. Pratt's death. Moira spent some time in the room, but that was more than a year ago. She could refuse them and search it herself, but they may well return with a warrant. Cooperating might also offer a chance to find out more about the body that is being examined in Oxford.

"Be my guest," she says, leading the way from the lodge. "What's the alleged crime?"

"Some missing property," says Lestrange. "It's probably just a crank, but we were in the neighbourhood and figured we could clear it up quickly if we popped in."

"Tell me," she says as they cross the quadrangle towards the dormitory building, "how did you conclude that there is no record of this Jane Doe? I can understand not having her fingerprints on file, but have you tested her DNA?"

"All in good time, lass," Lestrange says. "We only have DNA samples in the database for criminals, so it's not much use when identifying a young person if they've not had a run-in with the law. In most cases when we find a body, the person either has ID on them—a wallet or a phone—or someone reports them missing and identifies the body."

"And that hasn't happened here?"

"Not as far as I know. No one's come forward and we haven't found a purse or even a set of keys."

"That's quite enough, Constable," Inspector Bradstreet cuts him off. "You will recall that we are here to investigate, not to gossip."

"Very good, Inspector." Lestrange bows his head slightly, mollifying his superior.

They climb the stairs of the dormitory building and she opens her door.

"Is it all right if we look around a little?" Lestrange asks, ever polite but also establishing her consent to the search.

Even as she waves them in, she knows that something is wrong. It is too late to send them away, but someone else has been in her room. The stacks of paper on her desk are a little too randomly arranged. The drawer is a quarter inch more open than when she left an hour ago. She walks over and puts her hand on the chair—still warm.

There are only two practical hiding places in the room, but the closet is open and there is no one under the bed. He or she—probably she—has left.

Lestrange appears to have a semblance of a plan, running his fingers down the shelves of her bookcase. But Bradstreet is merely glancing about, as if waiting for something.

"If you tell me what you are looking for, I might be able to assist?" she asks.

"Nah, it's probably just a wild goose chase," Lestrange says, crouching to look under the bed.

Bradstreet, meanwhile, strides purposefully towards the desk and opens the drawer. He is not searching; he is following instructions. "Oh yes, Lestrange? Well, the sauce for the goose is sauce for the gander. What do we have here?"

"I'm not sure that's how the phrase is used, sir—" Lestrange swallows the rest of the sentence as he sees what the other officer is holding.

Triumphant, Inspector Bradstreet lifts the black velvet pouch from inside her desk. Tilting it to one side, an octagonal gemstone about the size of a large grape rolls onto his open hand. He holds it up to the window, the dazzling blue catching fragments of the winter sunlight. His eyes, glinting also, move from the stone to focus on her. "Care to explain yourself?"

A theft to distract Magnus, but also to implicate her? If Moira has planted the stone here, what does the other her achieve? She hardly needs to get Arcadia's attention. Is this Moira's way of saying that she is guilty after all? Guilty of what?

"St. Edward's Sapphire, I presume?" she says innocently. "I saw it once when we visited the Tower."

Bradstreet cannot stop the smile spreading across his face. "We're onto you this time, Miss Greentree."

Juveniles are not normally handcuffed when arrested, but Bradstreet takes out a pair and dangles them in front of her nonetheless. "You're coming with us, young lady— you're nicked."

4
MISDIRECTION

"My poor, dear, Arcadia. In the prime of her youth, a promising future ahead of her—all for naught as she turns to a life of crime. Such a waste."

"Thanks for the moral support, Magnus," she says, rolling her eyes. "As ever, you are a pillar of strength."

"Always happy to help my baby sister. Or at least, the sister with whom I was raised. Speaking of which, may I?" He gestures at her arm and she lifts the sleeve to reveal his signature. He nods with satisfaction. "One can't be too careful." Once fooled by Moira, he seeks to avoid falling into a cliché.

From the freedom side of the bars, Magnus looks around the holding cell and sniffs with disapproval. "I must say, it's a good thing you called me rather than a lawyer. With luck, we'll have you out of here before supper. Just as well, for I gather the food is most unsavoury."

"You seem very confident of that," Inspector Bradstreet

says from the doorway. He has been waiting for at least a minute, seeking a dramatic entrance. Constable Lestrange follows him into the custody suite, his own face suggesting a twinge of embarrassment at the Inspector's theatrics.

"Are you referring to my assessment of this facility's cuisine or my sister's imminent release?"

Bradstreet rises to the bait. "Your sister, here, was the last person to see not one, not two, but *three* teachers at her school before they died. And now we find her in possession of one of the most valuable jewels in the world, recently stolen from the Tower of London. I don't think she's going anywhere—and I don't particularly care if she finds our 'cuisine' to her fancy."

"Oh come now, Inspector," Magnus switches easily into the tone of supplicant. "I fear we got off on the wrong foot. Perhaps you would care to explain to me how you came by this intelligence that led a deeply underestimated police officer in a sleepy part of England to solve one of the crimes of the century?"

Uncertain whether he is being made fun of, Bradstreet straightens his jacket and tilts his head back. He has read a pamphlet on body language and believes that this posture makes him look intimidating. It does not. "I don't need to explain myself to you," he says.

"No, but you will need to explain yourself to someone when you are revealed to have been played for a fool."

"What are you talking about?" Inspector Bradstreet's head resumes its normal position, but his Adam's apple bobs up and down—unfeigned evidence that he is anxious.

"I am saying," Magnus says slowly, "that you have been tricked into arresting my sister and that if you put in a formal report of this matter you will soon be the laughing stock of Her Majesty's Constabulary. That's why I'm here: to help you."

"To help m— *me*?" Bradstreet sputters, beginning to turn purple.

"Inspector, the tip you received. I'm guessing it was anonymous and untraceable. And I am also guessing that it told you exactly where to find the jewel. Do stop me if I'm mistaken?" The Inspector's silence indicates that he is not. Her brother nods with satisfaction. "Now, there are two ways that another person would know that said jewel was in my sister's desk. Either they saw her put it there, or they put it there themselves. Let us take the first scenario: how could they have seen her put it in the desk drawer?"

"I don't know and I must say I don't particularly care," Bradstreet declaims. "Maybe she bragged about it. Said something on the phone. Or Facebooked about it on YouTweet."

"I think you mean posted something on social media, sir," Lestrange corrects helpfully, earning a scowl.

"Yes, all of that is possible, I suppose," Magnus concedes. "But really, does my sister strike you as the kind of person to make such an elementary mistake? Or, indeed, to have many friends either in real life or in the virtual world?"

"Thanks a *lot*, Magnus," she says. But her brother is leading Bradstreet towards the obvious deduction. The trick is to make him think he has reached it himself.

Magnus flashes her a winning smile. "One shouldn't *count* one's friends," he says in mock earnestness. "It's more important to have a few friends one can count *on*." Allowing the cereal-box wisdom to sink in, he addresses Bradstreet. "I'm sure you see my point, Inspector Bradstreet. The obvious inference is..." He allows his voice to trail off expectantly.

Like a trained seal, Bradstreet tries to balance the ball upon his nose: "Yes, well, clearly it is *possible* that whoever tipped us off put the gem there. Even if that were the case, however, being in possession of such stolen property still makes your sister a person of interest in the case."

"Ah yes, the jewel itself," Magnus gives an exaggerated sigh. "I very much regret that you may have been misled in that area also."

"What do you mean?"

"If my hypothesis that the jewel was planted is correct, it beggars belief that the true perpetrator would part with a priceless stone simply to inconvenience my sister in the weeks before Christmas."

Bradstreet looks puzzled, so Magnus restates it more simply: "I mean that you found *a* gem, but I am not sure you found *the* gem. Would it be possible to have a look at it?"

"A look?" Bradstreet turns to Lestrange, incredulous. "Does he think this is some kind of game?"

"No indeed, but in about"—Magnus casts a glance at the clock on the wall—"one minute, the station phone is going to ring with the Commissioner of Scotland Yard asking how cooperative you are being in my efforts to help you. All things considered, I believe it would be best for both of us if the answer is a simple 'very'."

Bradstreet looks from Magnus to her and back again. His eyes narrow as his brain ticks over the possibilities. Then his jaw sets in a sign of determination. "Just how stupid do you two think I am?"

From within the cell she cannot resist: "Do you really want to know?"

"Now, now, Arcadia," Magnus intervenes. "Let us remain civil." He turns back to Bradstreet. "I do realise that I am putting you in a difficult position, but believe it or not I really am trying to help."

The sincerity in her brother's voice is almost perfect. Almost. But will it be enough to sway Bradstreet?

The Inspector is weighing his options when a chirping noise announces an incoming telephone call on the station's official line. No one moves, but Magnus is finding it hard to resist a smile of anticipation.

After a third ring Lestrange lifts the receiver. "Hello?" He listens for a moment, back straightening noticeably as he does. "Yes, just a moment, sir." He stretches out the receiver to the Inspector wordlessly.

Bradstreet snatches it and brings it to his ear. "Bradstreet here," he barks. "Yes? Commissioner? Well, it's very good to hear from you also." His eyes dart from Magnus to her as he listens. "Of course I'm grateful for the assistance." Then his eyes close in resignation. "Naturally, we're offering every accommodation." His shoulders fall in defeat. "No, thank *you*, Commissioner."

He hands the receiver to Lestrange, who returns it to the wall. "Go on then," he snaps, "get it from the evidence room."

"Very good, Inspector." Lestrange bustles off.

The tapping of Bradstreet's foot is the only sound until Lestrange returns with the black velvet pouch and hands it to him. The Inspector reaches inside and carefully removes the octagonal gemstone, looking at it suspiciously.

"May I, Inspector?" Magnus asks gently, extending a soft palm.

After a second's delay, Bradstreet places it in her brother's hand. His fingers close around it like so many sausages and he takes a silk handkerchief from his pocket to wipe it down fussily. He then approaches the duty sergeant's desk, on which a cup and saucer from a recent tea-break rest. Setting the cup aside, Magnus places the gem in the centre of the saucer.

"As I'm sure you know, Inspector," he says, "sapphire— also known as corundum—is the second hardest mineral on the Mohs scale."

Despite irritation at being forced to cooperate, the

flattery hits its mark. "Sure," Bradstreet says gruffly. "The hardest would be diamond."

Magnus beams at him. "Excellent! I see you are a fellow aficionado." From his pocket he produces a small glass bottle. "I happen to have brought with me some acetone—a simple organic solvent that you might find in nail polish remover or paint thinner. To a real sapphire, it should be completely harmless."

"Now just wait a minute—" Bradstreet blurts, realising what he is about to do. But Magnus moves with unusual fluidity, emptying the clear liquid over the stone. It fills the saucer, a sweet fruity smell wafting through the air. Bradstreet's hand is halfway to the stone but he stops, watching in fascination.

From her position in the cell it is hard to see, and for a moment nothing happens. Bradstreet clears his throat, a triumphant witticism on the tip of his tongue. Then the liquid begins to change colour, leeching it from the stone. Bradstreet's open mouth, poised to speak, simply gapes as the stone lists to one side. Within a minute it sinks further, submerged in the acetone, now blue, as the sapphire dissolves like an over-priced lozenge.

"What have you done?" Bradstreet whispers, having at last regained control of his jaw.

"What have I done?" Magnus replies cheerfully. "Why, I've saved you the trouble of filling in tedious forms about a non-existent crime." He picks up the saucer and carefully pours the liquid into the cup. "Just as I thought: it was

Lucite—a type of plastic. Oh don't feel bad, Inspector. This substance has been used to make costume jewellery for almost a hundred years. Now, what do you say to letting my sister smell the fresh air of freedom once again?"

She had decided earlier to phone Magnus not out of desperation but curiosity. For Moira to steal the jewel and then have her arrested made little sense. And, in relation to the sapphire in particular, her brother had access to more information than was at her disposal.

"I will come post-haste," her brother said easily when she reached him. "Though I fear I'm in the midst of some rather pressing matters; I shall be with you before the end of the day."

She ignored the invitation to ask what was more pressing than his sister's incarceration and resigned herself to an afternoon of introspection. When, a mere thirty minutes later, the call of "visitor" echoed through the custody suite, it seemed unlikely that her brother had hastened his arrival. In addition, the footsteps were of leather soles on the linoleum; her brother preferred rubber, putting comfort ahead of fashion.

"Dr. Bell?" she said as the Oxford physician was ushered through. "This is an unexpected pleasure."

"Ah, yes," he replied. "I don't mean to, er, intrude." His thinning hair was askew, absent-minded fingers running through it. He was preoccupied with something, presumably the reason for his visit.

"Not at all," she said. "I must apologise that I am not really in a position to offer you much in the way of hospitality. But perhaps I can assist you with your inquiry?"

"My inquiry?" Dr. Bell repeated.

"I doubt you would have travelled all the way to the Priory School and then obtained information about my current location without a pressing reason. To come in person suggests a matter of some sensitivity. Possibly you wish to share some news, but more likely you have a discreet query?"

He shook his head as if baffled. Then nodded, a combination of movements that left his hair in rebellion against his scalp. "Yes, I visited your school. Are the students always quite so—unruly? It took some time before I could find a porter to assist me. He was most reluctant to part with the information as to your location, but I explained that I needed to see you about your Oxford interviews."

"You do?"

Dr. Bell dabbed at his mouth with a handkerchief. "I confess that I may have taken some liberties in giving the *impression* that it concerned admission to Oxford. Oh, rest assured: I am cautiously optimistic on that front. Assuming, of course, that the current"—he gestured vaguely to the cell bars—"unpleasantness can be resolved."

A glance out to where the duty sergeant sat at a nearby desk and he leaned in closer: "In fact, I wanted to speak with you about your twin sister—your late twin sister."

"The one who tried to kill us?"

"Er, yes, that one."

"What do you need to know?"

"As you might imagine, her spectacular demise threw something of a pall over our admissions interviews. And next week's Gaudy was almost cancelled. But, more importantly, I realised that we never had a chance to talk about what happened—and what this meant in terms of your quest to find your true identity."

"Not much, I fear. There's no record of Moira in the files that I've seen. And neither my brother nor I have had much success locating any information about her whatsoever."

"Ah yes, your brother. How is he these days?"

She laughed. "Magnus always lands on his feet. He's finished his studies—at the other place, I fear—and now works for the government."

"Good, good," Dr. Bell replied. "Though there is a resemblance, you cut a somewhat different silhouette than he."

A polite way of saying her brother is fat, which he is. "Magnus is of the view that life is uncertain and so one should always start with dessert, preferring not to wait until the end of a meal."

"While you disagree and, evidently, do some sort of cardiovascular exercise. Aerobics, perchance?"

"Boxing," she said, quietly, as the information was unlikely to help her in the eyes of the police.

"I see." Dr. Bell nodded. "An unusual choice for a young woman, but assuming you avoid head trauma and other injuries it offers a profitable fitness regime. *Mens sana in corpore sano.*"

"That's the hope," she replied. "A healthy mind in a healthy body. Though Magnus never quite accepted the connection. Actually, he's on his way here right now to try to help clear this up."

"Oh very good, very good," Dr. Bell said. "Now is there anything I can do myself to be of assistance? Having saved my life on multiple occasions, it surely behoves me to do what I can for you."

"That's kind of you, but I should be fine."

"Very well." He looked down at the watch on his wrist, winding it absent-mindedly until the coiled spring inside was at maximum tension. His eyes drifted up towards hers but he said nothing.

"Is everything all right, Dr. Bell?"

"Hmm?" Startled from his reverie, he blinked rapidly before looking away. "I'm sorry, Miss Arcadia. It's nothing. You remind me a little of my wife, that's all. She passed away many years ago. Long before you were born."

Was there a tear in his eye? If so, it was blinked away quickly. "Anyhow," he continued briskly, re-buttoning his coat. "I had best be off. The college will be in touch about admissions matters in January. All being well, I hope to see more of you in the coming months. Goodbye, Miss Arcadia."

It was only after he left that she realised she had not told him that Moira was still alive. Why? The urge to protect her sister only partly explained the dissimulation. If anything, she felt she was growing to trust Dr. Bell. And it was at that point that she realised she was starting to doubt herself.

Notwithstanding Magnus's prediction, even releasing her from custody apparently requires the filling in of various forms. On entry, as part of being processed, her bag was taken and put in a locked cabinet. It is now returned to her by a contrite Lestrange.

"I'm sorry about all this, Miss Greentree," he says.

"Oh don't worry," she replies. "I know you were just doing your job."

"Precisely," echoes Bradstreet. "I'm pleased to see that you accept this was a simple misunderstanding. Though"—there is a glint in his eye—"one upside is that we now have a record of you, with photograph, fingerprints, and DNA sample. You never know, perhaps that will come in handy one day?"

"Goodbye, Inspector." Magnus puts an arm on his sister's to steer her from the police station, even as he pre-empts a caustic reply.

She simply nods as they exit onto the street, where a navy blue Bentley is waiting for them. The engine starts as they approach and Magnus opens the rear door for her.

"Travelling incognito, I see?" she says, climbing into the luxurious interior.

"Needs must," her brother replies, sinking into the seat next to her.

"I suppose I should be thanking you for getting me released from jail."

Magnus taps the frosted glass panel separating them from the driver and the car glides away from the footpath. "I believe that would be customary."

"Thank you."

"You're most welcome."

They drive for a few minutes in silence, the main street giving way to country lanes en route to the motorway.

"So, I hate to admit it as much as you do," she says at last, "but I have no idea what Moira is up to."

Atypically, Magnus does not gloat but simply nods. "Indeed, it is more than a trifle disconcerting to deal with someone entirely rational and yet also entirely unpredictable." He adjusts a shade to keep the sun from shining in his eyes, a line of shadow crossing his face. "Possibly because of the unusual circumstances of her upbringing, Moira lacks not only the social graces but the very reference points of society. The means she adopts are perfectly logical, but they are in pursuit of ends that are themselves inscrutable. We can only try to deduce them in hindsight. Moira, on the other hand, appears to be prodigious at predicting the decisions of those around her."

She nods also. "In order to outwit someone who is able to predict your moves, it is necessary to choose differently—to act differently from how you would be expected to act. If that's possible."

"Indeed," Magnus says. "It reminds me of an old problem in which a game is played with a supercomputer said to possess the power of prediction. You are presented with two boxes: the first is opaque; the second is transparent and holds a thousand pounds. You are then asked whether you will take the contents of both boxes, or only the first box. The catch is that the machine claims to know what you are going to do—indeed, in hundreds of games with other players, it has never been wrong. And so, before you make your choice, the computer predicts whether you will take both boxes, or just the opaque one. If it predicts that you will take *both* boxes, the first box is left empty. But if the computer predicts that you will take only the *first* box,

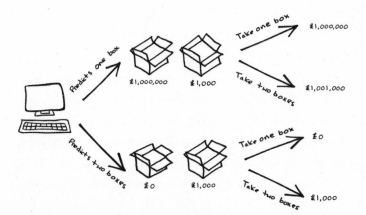

then it places a million pounds inside. So what do you choose?"

"We're assuming that I want to get as much money as possible, correct?"

"You can replace the cash with puppies, if you wish," Magnus says. "The principle remains the same. But yes, it is rational to maximise your return."

"And once the prediction has been made, the value in the first box will not change—regardless of what I choose."

"Correct. The prediction is final."

"So, rationally, if I want to maximise my return I should choose both boxes. Whichever prediction has been made, that brings me a higher return in each case. If the computer predicted that I would take both boxes, I get a thousand pounds instead of nothing; if it predicted I would take one box, I get a million pounds and an extra thousand."

"Yes," Magnus observes. "Your logic is impeccable." He waits.

She frowns. "But we're also told that the supercomputer has never been wrong. If we exclude the possibility of outwitting the machine, then we can rule out the scenarios in which I get either none or all of the money. So the choice is only between getting a million and getting a thousand pounds. In which case I should choose only the first box."

"Excellent. Once again, your logic is impeccable."

"Intriguing. And in this analogy Moira is the supercomputer?"

"That may be exaggerating slightly." Magnus takes two bottles of water from a recess in the car door and passes her one. "Though Moira has certainly demonstrated great capacity to predict and to plan. So the choice is whether to play her game or try to beat her at it. But beating her requires her to predict that you will not attempt to do so."

"I don't know, Magnus. Playing by her rules and getting a million pounds—or a million puppies—doesn't seem so bad. Is it worth risking all that for an extra thousand quid?"

"I accept that the analogy is not complete. But there are also principles at stake. Moira is operating completely outside the bounds of acceptability."

She stares at her brother for a moment. "You were never a great one for principles," she muses. Looking out the window, she sees the driver has missed the exit to the Priory School and is heading instead onto the M4. "Where are we going, Magnus?"

"Oh I just wanted to pop by a museum for a visit," her brother replies, a little too innocently. "I'll get you on a train back to school soon enough."

His sincerity will not fool her. Magnus's delay in coming to see her is suddenly cast in a new light. "I fear we might be a little late—doesn't that museum close at 4:30pm in winter?"

He simply chuckles.

"I must say," she observes, "that it was awfully lucky that the fake jewel was made of Lucite. It's a fairly antiquated form of costume jewellery. These days they tend to be made of glass or cubic zirconia. But if you poured a bottle of acetone over one of those, of course, the worst you would do is give it a good clean."

Magnus says nothing, but he is evidently pleased with himself. From a refrigerated compartment between the seats, he takes out a small cylinder of chocolates. "Salted caramel?" he offers, popping one into his own mouth at the same time.

"No thanks," she demurs. "But may I see it?"

Butter would not melt in her brother's mouth, but the salted caramel clearly does. "See what, Arcadia?" he asks around the liquid chocolate.

"The gem, St. Edward's Sapphire—the one you stole just now from a police station, switching it with a plastic copy that you then destroyed."

"Oh very well." He puts the chocolates back in their chiller and wipes his fingers clean on a wet cloth. Then from an inside pocket of his jacket, he retrieves the stone, wrapped in the silk handkerchief, and passes it to her.

"Impressive," she says, holding it up to the light. She leaves it to him to decide whether she is complimenting the stone or his exploits. "You delayed coming to see me so that you could have the copy made—or you acquired it from someone. Then procured the acetone—concentrated, I assume, to ensure a speedy disintegration of the Lucite. The switch was simplicity itself as you could turn your back on the marks as you put the fake jewel in the saucer. No offence, but I doubt you could have pulled it off relying only on sleight of hand."

"None taken," Magnus purrs. "Prestidigitation was never my cup of tea. Misdirection, on the other hand— misdirection I can work with."

They have entered London proper now. Ahead of them looms the iconic Tower Bridge, but the car takes a sharp left onto a siding that drops down below the elevated road. The Bentley slows at an arched gate that swings open as they approach. Headlights come on automatically as they drive into the tunnel, briefly illuminating the blackness that swallows the car and its occupants.

5
RAVEN

Her Majesty's Royal Palace and Fortress of the Tower of London was a residence before it was a prison. The White Tower still dominates the complex. Designed in the eleventh century primarily to keep Londoners hostile to their Norman rulers out, the rag-stone building's ability to keep prisoners in was called into question by its first detainee, who was also the first to escape. The flaw was more human than architectural, however. After he was locked up in 1100 AD for embezzlement, friends of Bishop Ranulf Flambard concealed a rope within a flagon of wine and sent it to him. The benevolent bishop threw a party, ensured that his captors drank copiously, and then used the rope to climb out a window when they had lapsed into a stupor.

The Tower fared better as a stronghold for the Crown Jewels, which—prior to Moira—had never been stolen. Colonel Thomas Blood came close in 1671, foiled when the Master of the Jewel House's son raised the alarm upon finding his father bound and gagged. As a result of Magnus's intervention, it seems that Moira's historic feat will be unrecorded.

The Bentley continues along the tunnel and through a second gate, taking them under the Tower grounds to pull up at a small underground carpark. Magnus alights, indicating for her to stay within the vehicle.

She watches her brother approach a solid metal door with multiple locks. As he nears, it opens and a stout Yeoman of the Guard steps out. Dressed in a uniform that has barely changed in five centuries, the beefeater's scarlet doublet has a white ruff and gold trim, scarlet tights covering his legs down to patent-leather shoes. The garish clothing somehow fits the sombre moment—a priceless jewel and symbol being returned to its rightful home.

As Magnus produces the pouch, the flat-brimmed black velvet hat bows in acknowledgement, also serving to shield the face of the guard from view. Two patient hands are extended to receive the jewel, but Magnus pauses.

The beefeater is short, no taller than herself, though it is decades since height restrictions were in place for British forces. The padded doublet conceals much of his body shape—if it is a "he" at all. Magnus turns to look over his shoulder at his sister: he suspects also. Not normally given to theatrics, her brother appears ready to make an exception in this instance. Moira has fooled him once too often and he is going to enjoy his revenge, a vindication of his superior powers of observation and proof that he is impervious to

Moira's dissimulation. With a flourish, Magnus raises his hand—and knocks the beefeater's hat clear from her head.

No, on reflection, definitely *his* head.

She estimates the balding pate to be that of a fifty-year-old man. From Cornwall, if she were pressed for a county. Had he not been bald, of course, the shock of being attacked by Magnus might have caused alopecia to reveal his shiny scalp anyway. Instead, he simply gasps and staggers back, fear and confusion in his eyes.

Magnus is profuse in his apologies—misunderstanding, been under a lot of stress, no harm done. She is too far away to hear the words, but the meaning is clear in her brother's posture. After a minute of this, the hat gently dusted down and restored to its rightful place, the beefeater is mollified and bows once more. With less grandiosity, Magnus hands over the velvet pouch with the jewel and returns to the car.

"Not a word," he says tersely.

But she cannot resist. "Perhaps you would like to sign his arm also?" she inquires innocently.

"Oh do shut up, Arcadia." He leans forward to tap on the partition and their unseen driver takes them further into the darkness.

The Bentley emerges on the other side of the Tower complex, winding a path through London's labyrinthine streets. She does not bother to ask the destination; it will become clear soon enough.

Taxi drivers who ply these roads on a daily basis must famously acquire "The Knowledge", memorising some 25,000 streets and countless possible routes. Studying can take two to four years, during which the hippocampus—the seahorse-shaped part of the brain used in spatial memory—grows measurably. Storing so much information comes at a cost, however, and some cabbies have diminished short-term memory as a result.

Magnus's driver is following a well-travelled route, changing lanes in advance of turns and without hesitation. Or perhaps he is using a satellite navigation system.

The car follows the Thames for a while and approaches Canary Wharf, stopping outside a nondescript glass and steel office building. Magnus alights, this time holding the door open for her. They enter the building, where a security guard sits behind a desk below the minimalist logo of Universal Exports Ltd. He nods at Magnus as they walk towards a bank of elevators. There are no buttons, though a door opens as they approach.

"'Universal Exports'?" she says as the lift doors close.

"Lighten up, Arcadia," Magnus replies stiffly. "If it was good enough for Mr. Bond I'm sure it will be fine for our purposes. Besides, there really is an import-export company in this building, with a thriving business in casual sportswear. Above ground, that is all that any observer would see."

There are no buttons in the cabin either, but it starts to descend.

"Below ground," he continues, looking pleased, "is a different story."

Universal Exports Ltd. is the cover used by Britain's most famous fictional spy, James Bond. The existence of the agency for which he works—MI6, also known as the Secret Intelligence Service—was officially denied by the British government until 1992, well after the release of the sixteenth film popularising his exploits. Was the choice of cover here some inside joke among the spies? Or an elaborate ruse to give the appearance that it was an MI6 facility when in fact it hosts some other organisation?

After a descent of fifty feet or so, the doors open. Another guard at another desk nods at them, a curiously familiar form of security. Unless there are unseen scanners, the number of people entering the facility must be reasonably small. Or it might be that Magnus's distinctive figure makes a formal identity check redundant.

The second guard's desk lacks a corporate logo, nor are there signs indicating what lies down the corridors that lead off from the anteroom. Magnus goes to the left and she follows, entering a conference room with dozens of screens displaying security camera footage from around London. On another wall a stream of social media posts float up like bubbles in a soda. Each apparently chosen according to some algorithm, it is like hearing snippets of conversation at a café—a café in which all the talk is of bringing down the government or rising up in violent revolution.

She is reminded of her former Headmaster's secret

chamber with its video feeds from around the school. Magnus passes through the conference room and into another hallway. Analysts at desks with laptop computers pore over data ranging from bank transfers to browser histories, the electronic footprints of modern life. At the end of the corridor is a large office with glass walls, an ornately carved desk and overstuffed leather chair incongruous in the high-tech environs. On the desk— oak, it appears—an antique globe sits next to a fountain pen and blotter.

Magnus approaches the office—and then sits down at a small cubicle just outside it. A raised eyebrow dares her to say something. She declines to do so.

She borrows a chair from the adjacent cubicle, noting the takeaway pizza box poking out of its dustbin. "So," she says at last. "I assume you didn't bring me here to impress me. Have you decided that you do in fact need my help, not merely to serve as bait? Am I getting warm?"

Magnus is looking down, busy with something in his desk drawer, but a grunt indicates she should continue.

"The files Moira accessed in your system," she says. "You can't work out what she was looking for, or why she stole what she stole. You think I can help."

When her brother lifts his head he is holding a muffin. "Not quite. You see, she didn't steal anything. Nor did she access the most sensitive files." He takes a bite from the muffin—banana by the smell. "Based on what we have been able to reconstruct, she was particularly interested in the suppliers for the project. I was rather hoping you might assist us in working out why."

Putting the muffin down, Magnus taps on a keyboard and a list of names and organisations appears on the screen set into his cubicle. Some are large technology companies like Apple and IBM, but there are also a dozen or so individuals; on a line by itself, one is identified simply as "X". She recognises two of the names, one of them belonging to a dead man. Lysander Starr is listed as a consultant at Reading University; a column indicates his status as "inactive". Something of an understatement. Directly above him in alphabetical order is Lucian Smythe, the fellow at Magdalen College who interviewed her only yesterday. He, by contrast, is "active".

Starr was a biological anthropologist. Smythe is a mathematician working on artificial intelligence. What kind of research project would bring them together?

Not enough data. "I would love to help you, brother dear," she says. "But it would help to know a little more about your pet project here. Something involving the interface between artificial intelligence and the human brain. Please don't tell me that you've been trying to build a friend to play chess with."

Magnus yawns. "You know perfectly well that there are more than adequate chess programmes on the open market. In any case, I'm much more interested in wetware than software."

One of the other companies on the list is GE

Healthcare, indicated as a provider of fMRI. Functional magnetic resonance imaging is used to map brain activity and diagnose neurological problems. Gather enough information about the brain's workings, upload it into a sufficiently powerful computer, and— "You're modelling artificial intelligence on an actual brain? Making a copy of someone's neural activity and running it on a computer? I didn't think that was possible."

"It is not. Yet," Magnus concedes. "And though you have essentially guessed the outlines of Project Raven— albeit after more than enough time and clues—I must warn you that you are still bound by the Official Secrets Act not to speak of this with anyone else."

"'Project Raven'?"

"It seemed like a good idea at the time." Magnus takes another bite of the muffin. "After the poem by Edgar Allen Poe."

"'Once upon a midnight dreary'," she quotes. "I know the poem. But what is the connection with brain scans?"

Magnus sniffs, feigning disappointment even as he revels in the opportunity to explain the allusion. "The poem, as you recall, is about a young man struggling to forget his dead lover, Lenore. Wallowing in self-pity, his reverie is disturbed by a 'stately raven', which shows that he will never forget Lenore."

"I thought the raven was a metaphor for his descent into madness?"

"Well, that's another interpretation." The remainder of

the muffin disappears into her brother's mouth. "In any event, the project aims to capture memories by taking a snapshot of the brain. It's true that computers cannot yet match the brain in terms of raw power. Machines may outperform humans in most tasks, but that's because people—most people, at least—use their brains so inefficiently. A supercomputer might have billions of transistors, each with three connections to other transistors. The human brain has a *hundred* billion neurons, each connected to up to ten thousand other neurons.

"Give a machine a clear task and the machine wins. Calculators surpassed mental arithmetic in the 1960s; chess was more complicated and so humans held out until the 1990s. The Chinese game *go* is even trickier, though computers now win at that also. But give a computer something really hard—like recognising faces or processing natural language—and a child will still outperform it. Maybe in another decade or so our silicon friends will catch up with us. In the meantime, the Raven mapping process lets us capture and analyse the state of the brain—reconstructing, for example, the last moments of a dying soldier's life."

"Or interrogating a prisoner," she adds. "You wouldn't even need to ask him a question."

"Such intelligence-gathering possibilities have not escaped our attention." Once again, Magnus busies himself at the desk drawer. This time he emerges holding a muesli bar between his forefinger and thumb, as if it were toxic. "My secretary occasionally slips these in, telling me that they are 'healthy'. I think she means 'healthful', but such seed-based confections are clearly intended for birds and not humans." He drops the offending object in the dustbin next to the empty pizza box.

"And why do you think Moira is interested in your little project here?"

"I believe, sister dear, that you previously deduced that this is what *I* wanted to ask *you*."

Very well. "Starr's name cannot be a coincidence," she begins. "Perhaps Moira is trying to work out who else is connected to him, either to punish them for what they did to her or to find out the truth about her upbringing. Or maybe she wants to continue the experiment, to realise her full potential." She pauses. "Is there any way that your Project Raven could be directed to that end?"

A crease works its way across Magnus's brow. "I doubt it. The focus is on mapping and recording brain activity, not enhancing it." The crease deepens and his jaw sets a little more firmly. "I did explore, for example, whether the technology could be used to help coma patients recover from brain trauma. Unfortunately all it offers is a more rigorous diagnosis—not a cure."

The image of Mother in her hospital bed comes unbidden. *Mens sana in corpore sano.* Focus on the matter at hand: if Moira could unravel who was involved in imprisoning her, it might also reveal the identity of the professor behind the attack on her parents.

"Who or what is 'X'?" She points to the single character at the bottom of the list. Instead of "active" or "inactive", the status is listed as "classified".

"Alas, there are secrets in this world to which not even I am privy," her brother replies. "'X' is one of the founders of the project. I have not met him or her—statistically it is more likely to be a 'him', though I have learned not to prejudge such matters. But I have been assured by the highest authority that he or she can be trusted completely."

"I didn't think you trusted anyone completely," she retorts. "What about Lucian Smythe. He's a fellow at Magdalen College and interviewed me only yesterday. I first met him a year ago and he outlined his theory of artificial intelligence—a kind of inverse Turing Test in which a computer doesn't try to fool a human into thinking it is conscious, instead the machine must fool itself."

A few taps at the keyboard and Magnus pulls up a personnel file. "Dr. Lucian Smythe," he reads. "Educated at Eton and Oxford, appointed Waynflete Professor of Pure Mathematics at Oxford two years ago."

"He's a professor?" she interjects. Smythe was introduced to her as a fellow at Magdalen.

"Yes," Magnus scans through the file. "One of the younger to hold that particular post, but mathematicians do tend to burn out quite early." He looks at her curiously. "Oh, I see that you're still looking for *that* professor. But you told me that he or she taught both Starr and the

woman Sophia Alderman, also known as Phaedra. Dr.
Smythe is younger than both of them. It's not impossible,
but it does seem highly unlikely."

It is indeed a stretch, but she has vowed to explore all
possibilities, however slim. "What has he been doing for
your Project Raven?"

Magnus pores over the screen for a moment. "Relatively
abstract work looking into how a computer simulation
might process data vastly more complicated than that
system could contain. He's written some quite interesting
papers on Gödel's incompleteness theorem that we think
might have some useful applications."

"And do they?"

Magnus faces her. "In part. Yet we're still years from
a working prototype." He stands. "Let me investigate
Dr. Smythe further. In the meantime, we should get you
back to school. Having saved you from a life of crime, I
can't have Aunt Jean and Uncle Arthur accusing me of
undermining your education by encouraging truancy."

They exit the same way they entered, analysts ignoring
them, the guard nodding absently as they leave. A thought
turns over in her head as they ride the elevator back to
the surface. "If Moira wanted to get in and out of your
system undetected," she says as they cross the lobby to
where the Bentley is waiting outside, "don't you think she
would have done so?"

A check in Magnus's gait suggests that she has struck
a nerve.

"Is it possible," she continues, "that Moira broke into your system not to take information but to give it to you?"

"Or to draw attention to it," her brother finishes the thought. "And, in particular, to get me to draw *your* attention to it. Hmm. An intriguing possibility that I shall ponder." They have reached the Bentley and he opens the door for her, uncharacteristically chivalrous today. "The car will take you to Paddington Station. Let me think about this, but do drop me a note if, by some miracle, you come up with an idea before I do?"

She smiles, despite herself. "Goodbye, Magnus. And go eat your muesli bar—you saw very well that it has chocolate chips."

His lips curl upwards. "I confess that it is nice to have someone in the world who at least comes close to understanding me. Cheerio, Arcadia!"

He closes the door and taps twice on the roof. The Bentley glides away from the headquarters of Universal Exports Ltd., wending its way back into the London traffic.

It is at the second corner that she realises: the Bentley's acceleration is more hesitant, the lane changes less assured. The route is consistent with a journey to Paddington Station, but it is a different driver.

The partition separating the front cabin from the passenger compartment is opaque glass. A button would lower it, but she prefers to know whom she will confront before opening a door.

Phone Magnus? Difficult to do so without attracting the driver's attention. A text message then:

Magnus, driver switched? Planning to exit ASAP.

The reply comes in seconds:

Backup vehicles on way. Sit tight. M

Sit tight? Her brother must be trying to irritate her. The Bentley cruises alongside the Thames but is caught in the evening traffic, coming to a rest at traffic lights. She resolves to get to the station by herself and pulls gently on the door handle, which moves freely but does not unlatch the door. The child lock is engaged, meaning that the door can only be opened from the outside. She is about to see if the power windows have also been disabled when the partition between her and the driver is lowered.

As before, it is the shoulders she notices first, an actor's posture even as the driver turns to regard her. "Hello again, Arcadia," says the former substitute teacher who came to the Priory School to spy on her but saved her from Headmaster, later returning to warn her about Moira and almost getting killed by Lysander Starr.

"Hello Miss Alderman," she says. "Or Mr. Shampie, or

Phaedra, or whatever you would like to be called today."

"You can call me Sophia," the teacher replies. "Phaedra was a name I never cared for."

"So what brings you back into my life now? If it's to warn me about my homicidal twin then I fear you're a day late."

The light changes to green and Miss Alderman—Sophia—directs the car forward. With the partition down, a muffled groan can be heard from the front seat. A faint odour of burnt clothing floats in the air. A look confirms that the original driver has been tasered and now lies incapacitated in the front passenger seat.

"He'll be fine," the teacher says over her shoulder. "And no, I'm not here to warn you about Moira. It seems that I have misjudged her all along. In her own peculiar way, she seems set on trying to help you. But you must know that she's not your twin—at least, not in the sense that you mean."

In the distance, police sirens blare against the rush hour traffic. "And what sense would that be?" she asks.

"I mean it is true that she is your identical twin, but you weren't born at the same time."

The sirens begin to get closer. "This is what you came to tell me? Because I should warn you that those police cars are coming for you. Next time might you introduce yourself before carjacking my ride?"

"Oh Arcadia," Miss Alderman—it is simpler to think of her as that—says. A look in the rear view mirror and she spins the wheel to the right, turning sharply down a narrow side street. "I did want to warn you, but not about Moira." The V8 engine of the Bentley roars as they accelerate, tyres squealing as the heavy vehicle manoeuvres around a corner. The sirens are now accompanied by the protesting horns of cars they have cut off or nearly hit.

"I don't think it's realistic to outrun them," Arcadia warns. "There is almost certainly some kind of tracking device in this vehicle, perhaps more than one."

At the wheel, Miss Alderman's face, reflected in the mirror, registers determination but also uncertainty. They may need only a few moments together, but it will be hard to talk while evading the police.

"Find a carpark," Arcadia says. "The tracking device is most likely linked to a two-dimensional map of London. If you can get into a multi-level carpark they will be able to follow you to the area but won't know which level you are on. Cameras will spot you going into the parking lot, but they aren't normally present on every level."

A raised eyebrow in the mirror. "Not bad," Miss Alderman says. "Let's just hope you keep using your powers for good rather than evil." The car swerves again as the teacher sees a carpark and veers onto the ramp. A screech of metal on concrete accompanies their entrance, the Bentley's front corner scraping against a wall. "Oops. I hope you're insured," Miss Alderman says, looking down at the incapacitated driver as she puts her foot down.

After climbing three levels, the Bentley slows and

comes to a halt near a lift lobby. Miss Alderman's hands on the steering wheel are white; a sheen of perspiration glistens on her brow.

"You should go," Arcadia says. "I'll put in a good word for you, but you did taser a government employee and steal and crash their car."

"I can't always be running away from you, Arcadia," the teacher says. But unbuckles her seatbelt nonetheless.

"What did you come here to tell me?"

Sirens now echo in the carpark. They have a minute, possibly less.

Miss Alderman reaches over the lowered partition to take her hand. "Arcadia," the teacher says, looking her in the eye. "There's so much I want to tell you, but I don't know if there will ever be time. So let me just say what I need to: stay away from Joseph Bell. He's trouble. The man has ruined too many lives already. Don't let him ruin yours."

Dr. Bell?

Miss Alderman opens the door and steps out of the car. She does the same and for a moment considers going with her former teacher. Yet they both know she can do more to help by staying with the car.

"Will I see you again?"

For the first time a flush of colour appears on the teacher's face. "I think so, Arcadia. I hope so."

And with a last lingering look, the substitute teacher, actor, and more enters the fire escape beside the lift lobby to flee from her side once again.

6
DISCIPLINE

It is late by the time she returns to the Priory School. The burly agents sent by Magnus questioned her multiple times about the attack on her driver, doubtless hoping that each new round of inquiries would prompt a fuller response. She replied—through breaths caught short to give the appearance of being near tears—that the man (or perhaps it had been a woman) wore a hat that covered his features. When the carjacker realised that they were being followed, he (or she?) turned into the carpark and fled on foot. No, she did not know why someone might have wanted to kidnap her. No, she could not help them identify him as she never saw his face. More short breaths, a welling of tears, and a request to pause for a moment as it was all too much.

Eventually, Magnus intervened and said he would arrange another car to take her back to the Priory School. "A *substitute* car, if you like," he added drily. Trusting that she had reasons for keeping Miss Alderman's involvement secret, he seemed satisfied with revealing to her that he, at least, knew the truth—even as he kept it from his colleagues.

As the car enters the school driveway, she stifles a yawn. The day is catching up with her; the prospect of her dormitory bed inviting. When she reaches the gates, however, it is clear that something is amiss. A distressed Mr. McMurdo shifts about in the lodge, some internal conflict causing his whole body to tense.

"Good evening, Mr. McMurdo," she says. "I'm sorry to be so late, but I gather my brother called ahead?"

"Aye, Miss Greentree. Though there's nowt respect for rules these days 'n all. 'Taint right," he mutters. "'Taint right."

"What do you mean?" Earlier, he shared his concern about students taking over school discipline, but now seems more agitated. He wants to act on some infraction but has been told not to? She tries a gambit to test her theory: "What has Sebastian been up to?"

A raised eyebrow confirms her suspicions. She nods, encouraging the porter to speak.

"Our Mr. Ormiston, he's a good man," Mr. McMurdo begins. "But I'll be damned if I can understand why he's done left the students in charge. An' this evenin', with the teachers out at their dinner 'n all, the students have been runnin' amok. I keep peace as best I can, but our Mr. Ormiston made me swear not to interfere unless there was threat to life 'n limb."

The porter absently sorts some incoming mail into pigeon-holes. "Eighteen years 'n more I've been working here, afore you or your brother, even afore that no good Milton came here—devil take 'im. I ain't seen nothin' like this."

She nods again. "And Sebastian?"

"Well, Master Harker's living it up like he were lord of the manor, ain't he just? Yellow card this, yellow card that. An' poor little blighters like Arty Saltire are the ones who get it."

"Get what?"

"Punished. Extra duties an' the like he can take. But the abuse is downright mean. Cruelty, that's what it is, pure n' simple."

Mr. McMurdo has long seen himself as a stand-in for the absent parents of many of the students. He is particularly protective of those who have lost a mother or father, like her, and those whose parents seem to regard boarding school as more of a lifestyle choice than an educational one. Arthur Saltire falls into the latter category—Henry also. Such parents dutifully visit on appropriate days and collect their wards at the end of term, but there is a discernible lightness in their departure when the fruits of their loins are left to ripen in someone else's care.

"An' it ain't just Master Harker," the porter continues. "He's a bad influence on all around him. The meanness that's comin' out is unhealthy, I tell you. An' now he says he's got somethin' special planned for tomorrow. I don't like it. Not one little bit."

There does not seem to be much more to learn at this point. "Thanks, Mr. McMurdo," she says. "I'll keep an eye on Arthur." As the words leave her lips, she recalls Mr. Ormiston asking her to promise something similar. Curious.

She collects the mail from her own pigeon-hole and crosses the darkened quadrangle to the dormitory building and her rooms. It is past lights out, but rules are now guidelines at best. Without even bothering to draw the curtains, she switches on a reading lamp and sits in the chair by her window. As the kettle boils, she takes Mother's diary from the bookshelf and opens a page at random. It is one of the earlier entries.

22 July 2000—Oh my goodness she's so different from Magnus. That boy would wake every two hours and demand to be fed, screaming his outraged end-of-the-world cry until he got what he wanted. Some days I was so tired I thought about crashing the car so I could at least close my eyes. I knew it was crazy, but being sleep-deprived can make you a little batty.

With Arky, she just lies there looking up at the ceiling, at the mobile, at me. The doctor thinks I'm imagining it but she seems to be doing more than

daydreaming. There's nothing sinister, but it looks—
the only way I can describe it is that it looks like she
has a secret. Maybe she does.

If there was any such secret, she has no recollection of
it. Hardly surprising, since the absence of language makes
it difficult for the brain to store memories at seven months.
The entry goes on to describe Mother's introduction of
solid foods.

On food, too, they couldn't be less alike. Magnus
never saw a calorie he didn't take a shine to. But
Arky suddenly became very fussy when I started
weaning her. I was following that Ford woman's
advice, but Arky was so picky. She seemed to enjoy
broccoli but then turned her nose up at peas. Sweet
potato was fine but then carrots were all flung to the
floor. Afterwards I tried kiwi fruit, banana, apple,
parsnip, pear—each and every one found a path to
the ground. Sometimes she would hold the food out
from her high chair and look at me, waiting for me
to make eye contact or say something before she
dropped it. Never in anger.

Then I tried watermelon and she gave me a big smile,
mashing it into her gums with the two white teeth
poking out.

In the end, it was Magnus who spotted the pattern.
So I went back to peas, then banana, then capsicum.
The next day it was melon, parsnip, and strawberry.
As long as I went in the cycle green, yellow, red,
she was happy. And I realised that these were the
colours of the traffic lights in her favourite book and
of the pedestrian crossing near our home. Magnus
said we should blindfold her during dinner as an
experiment, but I thought that was a bit much.

She has read all this before, but the echoes of Mother's
voice still make her smile. She flicks ahead to a moment
that was evidently a source or relief as well as frustration
to Mother, who had been anxious about when she would
begin to speak.

17 March 2001—Words at last! After all my anxiety
it was Ignatius who heard them. Arky woke from a
nap when he came home from work. He changed her
nappy and put her on the ground. "Where is Mama?"
she said. "In the kitchen," he replied. And off she
tottered to come find me. Fool of a man went to
change out of his work clothes and only mentioned it
at dinner.

It is late and she has almost finished her peppermint
tea, but she treats herself to one more vignette from her
second year.

25 May 2001—I think they're having a laugh but Ignatius swears black and blue that it happened. Magnus was playing chess against him when Arky sidles up and starts watching them. Ignatius isn't as quick as Magnus and while he was thinking, Magnus went in search of cake. Ignatius makes his move and then Arky reaches out to the board and grabs Magnus's queen. Cake crumbs fly as Magnus cries out that she'll mess up the board, so Arky puts the queen down but on a different square.

"Hmph," Magnus says around another mouthful. "Queen to king's rook seven. Not bad, but hardly as elegant as knight to king's bishop six. Either way, checkmate, Father."

Poor Ignatius. He's used to losing to an eight-year-old, but it can't be good for a man's ego to lose to his daughter still in her nappy.

The diaries make no mention of Moira. Did Mother know about her at all?

It is not unusual for twins to be adopted out separately—Miss Alderman herself once described a study of such twins reared apart during her brief but eventful period as one of the Priory School's staff. Yet in their last encounter she said that Moira is not really her twin—or that they are identical but not born at the same time.

So is Moira a clone? Starr said that Moira's genes have been edited to enhance her intelligence. But the CRISPR technology they used was only developed in the past few years. Fear of "designer babies" led to an effective moratorium on human testing—when a Chinese lab announced two years ago that it had experimented on non-viable embryos, the major journals refused to publish its work due to worries about ethics.

Pieces of a jigsaw start to fall into place. Moira is intelligent, rational, knowledgeable. But no one would accuse her of being mature.

Another yawn forces itself from her mouth. She should sleep. One more diary entry. She opens a page towards the middle, from when she was three.

22 July 2003—So we tried out a new day-care place today. It didn't go well. One of the boys drew a big red X on the sunflower that Arky was painting. The teacher said she was amazed how well Arky took it, calmly starting over again. But at naptime, Arky pretended to sleep, waiting until the other children were dozing and the teachers having their break. Then she got up and used a permanent marker to write "I am a moron" on the boy's forehead.

I was called in and asked to make Arky apologise to the boy. "Why?" she protested. His parents were there also, the mother rubbing furiously at the words but only making the skin red and her son angry.

I said we apologise when we do something wrong. I tried to explain the difference between being clever and being wise, telling her the story about the clever children and the blind old woman. I'm not sure she understood it. Maybe she will in time.

"But I'm not wrong," Arky replied. "He's dumber than the other kids. And he ruined my painting. This warning is a public service. I should be thanked!"

The boy's father was, to say the least, unhappy. I told Arky that we also apologise to keep the peace. She thought about this for a moment, and then nodded.

"I'm sorry," she said gravely to the boy's parents, "that your son is a moron."

That girl will be the death of me. But oh, she does make me laugh!

She has no recollection of the episode itself, but she did change day care a few times before ending up in a Montessori children's house. And though she still doubts whether it is right to express emotions one does not feel, she did learn from Mother that tact means speaking the truth—but doing so kindly.

The story about the blind old woman she knows well, for it was one of Mother's favourites. For years she thought Mother had invented the story herself, but later came across different versions in different cultures. Why it resonated with Mother quite so much, she never completely understood. Perhaps Mother identified with the old woman, trying in her sightless way to pass on a message of wisdom to the precocious children who inhabited her house. Or perhaps Mother just thought it was a nice story.

She rises early the next morning, taking a walk in the woods that adjoin the Priory School. It is not her habit to walk for its own sake—to exercise she swims or works out with a punching bag—but she wants to clear her head. Henry once hid in these woods until she and Constable Lestrange found him. He fled after being pressured by the former Headmaster to spy on her. Is she trying to escape something also?

Why did Miss Alderman tell her to stay away from Dr. Bell? He is one of the few people who has tried to help her find out the truth about her parents. Yet the warning resonates with something—her own hesitation to tell him that Moira survived the fire.

She does not believe in intuition. Often she will see the solution to a problem in a flash, but there is always a rational basis for it. Except now. For the first time in her life, she feels that she is grasping at an answer without even knowing the question.

Maybe she didn't come to the woods to escape; maybe she came looking for something that is lost.

She does not find it.

By the time she makes it to Hall, most of the students have already helped themselves to breakfast. Cornflakes crunch beneath her feet as she scavenges in the kitchen for coffee. An oversized tin of instant is open next to a kettle, but she is not that desperate. Eventually she locates beans and filter paper to start a pot.

As hot water seeps into the coffee grounds, dissolving the organic acids and sugars, she surveys the detritus from breakfast—and, it seems, dinner. Three or four students appear to have started with grand plans of cooking spaghetti bolognaise, only to abandon it in favour of ham sandwiches. The kitchen's supply of fruit and vegetables remains largely untouched. In time, scurvy might help the students remember to eat their greens.

Bearing coffee and an apple, she enters Hall itself. Less than twenty-four hours into Mr. Ormiston's experiment, his optimistic view of human nature is already being tested. Remnants of the sandwiches remain on the tables, students are running about and shouting, and at the front of Hall, where teachers normally take their meal or preside over assembly, a large object sits under a tablecloth. A chair of some sort.

Henry sits glumly in a corner, trying to ignore the din. She moves to sit down opposite him. "So what did I miss?" she says, taking a bite from the apple.

He looks up, pleased to see her—but worried about something. "You're the master detective," he replies quietly. "Go on, then: detect."

She takes in the room. "All right then," she begins. "Since I left, Sebastian has attempted to take over the school. A pliant student body follows him because they are entertained or just happy to see any kind of change. But he has no plan and those around him are there because they want power, not because they want to serve. So a dinner that would require effort is abandoned in favour of self-service sandwiches, and washing up duties are pushed onto those who desire clean plates for the next meal. Hygiene is going to be a problem before nutrition—it can take weeks for scurvy to set in, but this place will attract the local mice within a few days."

On a nearby table, a sparrow pecks at a half-eaten bowl of cornflakes. It cocks its head briefly to regard them, and then resumes its meal.

"To maintain order," she continues, "Sebastian will be looking to entertain as well as to intimidate. So distractions from the disorder will be called for—bread and circuses. Am I getting warm?"

"Not bad. Where were you, anyway?"

She considers her response. "Magnus wanted to catch up on some family matters."

He knows she is not being entirely truthful—and that she knows that he knows. "Fine," is all he says.

She nods at the tablecloth at the front of Hall. The high back of the object beneath it resembles the ornate carved wooden chair that the former Headmaster, Milton, once used. Mr. Ormiston had it put in storage when he took over, preferring a less grandiose seat from which to preside over assembly. "What's with the chair? Is Sebastian planning to use it as a throne?"

"I don't think so," Henry replies. "They moved it in here last night—from Chapel, by the looks of it. Sebastian and a few of his mates were snickering about—"

A crash at the door causes him to turn his head. One of the huge oak doors has slammed shut as Sebastian, Joan Hardy, and a few other upper sixth students enter. Walking in front of them, prodded now and then by Sebastian to keep moving, is the diminutive form of Arthur Saltire. If he was cowed by the previous day's run-in with Sebastian, he now looks terrified.

Sebastian, by contrast, is beaming. Evidently enjoying himself, he leads Arthur up to the front of the room to stand beside the covered chair. The noise of their entry has caused silence to descend on the room; whispered comments now fade away as Sebastian looks about expectantly. Despite his intellectual limitations, he has a certain charisma—given family connections, he may well be on a path to political office. For the moment, however, he has a school to run.

The sparrow took flight when the party entered and now circles above him, confused by the windows and the artificial lights. Sebastian looks up, contemplating a swat at it, but the bird is out of reach. He returns his attention to the students before him.

"My friends," he begins, calling them to order. "I come before you with a heavy heart. Yesterday, I thought we had started something together, a movement that would unite us as a student body. Supporting each other, caring for each other." He has clearly written this out and memorised it; his voice projects well, though the delivery is a little stilted. His populism is not yet polished. "Yet there are some among us who would pursue only their own desires, putting self above others."

With an air of gravity, he gestures to the boy next to him. "Arthur here, for example." He rests a hand on Arthur's shoulder, which slumps as if under a weight. "Why don't you tell the good people here what you did?" In an exaggerated stage whisper, he adds: "Go on, Arthur. You'll feel better afterwards: the truth will set you free!"

Sebastian reaching out for Biblical authority is a bit rich, but of what sin is he accusing Arthur? The younger boy is on the verge of tears, but stammers something out.

"I'm sorry, we couldn't hear that," Sebastian says, almost gently.

"I took some food," Arthur repeats.

"You took some food," echoes Sebastian, nodding with satisfaction. "You took some food," and then his voice hardens, "after we *specifically* agreed that food is to be shared equally and eaten only in Hall. That is rule number 7, is it not?" He looks around the room and there are a few nods. Others are trying to work out if he is serious or if this is some kind of performance art.

"Yesterday afternoon he started issuing edicts," Henry whispers to her. "There's a WhatsApp group you can join to keep up."

It has always been clear that Sebastian has something of the petty dictator in him, but the speed with which he transformed—and was allowed to transform—is implausible.

Petty dictator or not, he is enjoying the role: "And what was the food that you stole?"

Arthur mumbles a response and produces a piece of torn packaging, from a breakfast cereal carton of some sort.

A few gasps can be heard, causing Sebastian to nod more vigorously. "Yes," he says, "Coco Pops. Breakfast of the gods, served at the Priory School only twice a year— Easter and Christmas."

Sebastian's holier-than-thou demeanour is undermined by pagan references, but the other students appear to be hanging on every word.

"And you"—Sebastian is gathering steam now—"you took the only carton and scoffed the lot." Turning back to his audience, he declaims: "We found him in his room, up to his armpits in the stuff! What are we to do with such a person?"

"Punish him!" one of the female students cries out. Ironically? No, it appears to have been serious.

She can sense Henry's frustration. "This is ridiculous," he says, a little too loudly. "Shouldn't we give him the benefit of the doubt? A chance to prove he's innocent?"

"No!" comes the reply. "Sentence first—verdict afterwards!" She cannot see the female student, but the voice is familiar.

Sebastian looks on with the air of a cat savouring the moment before it bites down on a mouse. "Perhaps," he hesitates, "perhaps we can be merciful. So why, Arthur, why did you steal the food?"

The younger boy looks up at him, a hint of hope in his eyes. "I was hungry," he says.

But Sebastian's face hardens. "There," he cries, "you heard it from the culprit himself, admitting that he stole the food." More nods around the room. "Now the question is how to punish him. Should we put him in the hole, or should we"—a pause as he tugs the tablecloth off the chair beside him—"*charge* him?"

There is silence as the chair is revealed. Immediately recognisable as the former Headmaster's, black Velcro straps have been attached to the arms and legs, with electrical wires running from them to a small control box.

"The 'hole' is a cupboard in the basement," Henry whispers, keeping his voice low enough for only her to hear. "Sebastian started threatening to lock people in it yesterday afternoon. This chair thing is new."

"Don't worry," Sebastian is saying to the crowd with the oily grace of a used car salesman. "Old sparky here doesn't pack enough of a jolt to do any real damage. After all, our beloved Headmaster said we had to avoid lasting injury. Provided you don't go above six on the dial"—he points to the control box—"my little friend here should be just fine." He pats Arthur on the head. "But sparky may help him remember to be more *considerate* in the future."

There is palpable excitement in the room. She has read about a study in which people were left in a room by themselves for fifteen minutes with nothing to do but think. The only distraction was to give themselves an electric shock. The vast majority preferred mild electrocution to being left alone with their thoughts. That was a troubling reflection on boredom, but the atmosphere in Hall is something far uglier.

"So I ask you again," Sebastian says, "does he get confinement in the hole? Or an appointment with old sparky?"

It is unlikely that Sebastian intends any real harm, but the whitening of Arthur's face suggests that his body is preparing for it nonetheless. When fear causes adrenaline to be released, blood flows into the muscles and away from the skin—preparing the body to flee or fight, as well as decreasing blood loss in the event of injury.

The students, for their part, appear to be enjoying this. "Charge him!" someone calls out, soon echoed by another. Within moments it has become a refrain: "Charge him! Charge him!" Whether they are serious or treating it as a kind of game, Sebastian takes it as endorsement and motions for Joan and the others to strap Arthur into the chair.

The boy allows his wrists and ankles to be bound—is he paralysed by fear or seeking to avoid punishment for resisting? Something is rotten in the state of Denmark.

Sebastian picks up the wires that lead from the control box and carefully attaches electric clips to each of Arthur's fingers. Is the current direct or alternating? If the power source is a battery in the control box, Arthur would barely feel it. But the wires also run down the legs of the chair and into a recess in the floor. Surely they aren't reckless enough to have connected it to the mains power?

"And now," Sebastian continues, "we need a volunteer to administer the punishment." He scans the room and his eyes come to rest on her. "Ah Miss Greentree, how good of you to join us. We did miss you so at last night's feast. Since you're not quite one of us, I don't think we'll ask you to play this role. But Henry, would you do us the honours?"

Henry squirms in his seat but has no intention of rising. "No thanks, Sebastian. I don't want to be any part of this. Why don't you just let Arthur be and we can get on with our breakfast?"

Sebastian clicks his tongue. "Oh Henry, it must be very lonely up there on the moral high ground. Someone else, then?" On a nearby table, Harriet Doran, the American student, is finishing her cornflakes. Sebastian settles on her. "Miss Doran, our Yankee Doodle Dandy, would you be so kind as to come up here?"

Harriet's shoulders tense. She is about to excuse herself but Joan Hardy is swiftly beside her, encouraging her up to the front of Hall as if it were part of some daytime television gameshow. A quiet girl who prefers the company of her smartphone, she is evidently uncomfortable in the limelight like this. Nonetheless, she allows herself to be led to stand beside Sebastian.

"Now," he says, passing her the control box. "You are in charge—so to speak." He laughs at his little joke, but is the only one who does. A cough. "Anyway, let's get on, shall we? Now remember, Miss American Pie, don't go above six on the dial."

Arthur looks from Sebastian to Harriet and back. "Please don't do this," he whispers.

"It's a little late for that." Sebastian shakes his head sadly. "Now admit your wrongdoing and apologise."

"I told you, I was hungry. I'm sorry," Arthur says in a low voice.

"Hmm. No, I'm afraid I'm not convinced," says Sebastian. "Are you convinced?" he asks the assembled students.

"No!" three or four of them reply. Placed there by Sebastian? But their sentiment is echoed by others. "Get on with it!" someone calls out.

"Tough crowd," Sebastian says to Harriet. "But maybe we should give them what they want. Just turn the dial up to the number you want and then back down to zero. One can hardly be felt. Shall we start at two?"

The human body is an imperfect conductor of electricity. The dial presumably increases the voltage, meaning that the amount of current increases also. A small amount of current would be imperceptible. As it increases, it would cause pain and muscle reaction.

"Ouch!"

"Sorry!" Harriet has turned the dial up to two but quickly brings it back to zero.

Sebastian's eyes go heavenwards. "Don't *apologise*," he admonishes Harriet. "We're teaching him a lesson, remember?"

Harriet nods uncertainly as Arthur squirms in his seat.

"Now, how about a more sincere apology, Arthur?"

"Go to Hell, Sebastian," the younger boy replies. Good for him, standing up to the bully.

"Oh dear," Sebastian exclaims in mock horror, "I don't think he's sorry at all! Harriet, perhaps you might try number three?"

She hesitates, and so Sebastian reaches over to turn the dial up himself. In the chair, Arthur's body shifts and another "Ouch!" escapes his whitened lips.

Sebastian turns the dial back to zero. "Let's try that again, shall we?"

"Fine, I'm sorry, now take these blasted clips off my fingers."

Sebastian regards the crowd before him. "Well, what do you think? Is that a sincere apology?"

"No!" a handful of students call. Some of them are beginning to crowd forward, seeking a better view.

"So what should we do?" Sebastian raises his hands in feigned confusion.

"Charge him! Charge him!" comes the refrain.

"Number four, I think," Sebastian says to Harriet.

Once more, she hesitates.

"Oh come on," the stage whisper returns, barely audible above the chanting. "Arthur will be fine. Just give them what they want."

Another second, and then the American turns the dial up to four and back to zero. In the chair, Arthur's shoulders rise and he starts to sweat.

Beside her, Henry is heating up also. "We can't let this go on," he says under his breath. "Sebastian isn't a complete lunatic, but Arthur could get hurt."

As the amount of current increases, the possibility of electrical burns or stopping his heart goes up also. But that seems an unlikely scenario. "Just wait," she replies.

"All right," Arthur is saying, "I'll say whatever you want me to say."

"But we don't want that, do we?" Sebastian intones.

"We want you to tell us the truth!"

"Give him another dose!" one of the yearlings calls out. "Come on, Harriet: charge him!"

Holding the control panel, Harriet looks around the room with a puzzled expression. Unaccustomed to attention she may be, but she is realising that with it comes influence and power. As Arthur slumps in his chair, she straightens.

"Charge him! Charge him!" the refrain continues.

Harriet's eyes narrow and she turns up the dial to five.

Another cry escapes Arthur's lips as the knob returns to zero. "OK fine." Now he sounds angry. "So I took the blessed Coco Pops. Can you take these off me now?"

"So at last he confesses in full!" cries Sebastian, triumphant. "Now what punishment do you think we should impose?"

Even before he finishes the sentence, the chant has resumed: "Charge him! Charge him!"

"You heard the people, Harriet," he says.

The American girl's mouth is now set. Without being prompted, she turns the dial—to six.

"Stop it, stop it!" shrieks Arthur as pain courses through his body.

Beside her, Henry is beginning to stand.

But Sebastian is not about to be interrupted. "I don't hear him apologising." His brow creases into a frown. "I wonder if he's even sorry. How might we make him sorry?"

"Charge him! Charge him!"

Harriet's eyes are glazed, and she turns the dial yet again—past the safety point—to seven.

In the chair, Arthur's body begins to shake uncontrollably. Hall fills with jubilant cheers as the students look on.

Henry has left his seat. "We've got to do something," he says.

"Very well." She stands also. "You take care of Harriet, I'll get Arthur."

They move to the front of Hall where Sebastian is smirking. But Harriet's face has lost its grim determination. She is trying to turn the dial back to zero. Is it jammed? Panic appears in her eyes and soon her own body is shaking also, but with fear.

"I can't—" Harriet begins. "I can't switch it off."

Henry is beside her and grabs the control box, even as Arcadia reaches Arthur. The boy's muscles are tensing uncontrollably, a froth of saliva forming on his lips as his eyes are clenched shut. She reaches for the clips attached to his fingers.

"Wait, Arcadia," Henry cries. "If you touch him you'll get electrocuted also."

"I very much doubt that," she says, putting a hand on Arthur's wrist to hold him while she removes the cords from one finger at a time.

Arthur stops shaking and slumps forward in the chair. Sweat has discoloured his shirt and gradually his breathing returns to normal. Henry moves beside her; in a burst of heroism he rips the cords out from the control box, which he still holds. Behind him, Harriet is in tears while Sebastian looks on, untroubled.

From the back of Hall a loud voice calls out. "Very well, ladies and gentlemen, I think I'll take it from here."

Still in the chair, Arthur raises his head to look at Mr. Ormiston. "Is the game over, then?" he asks weakly.

"Yes it is, Arthur," Mr. Ormiston replies, walking towards the front of Hall, a mix of emotions on his face. Disappointment, mostly. He reaches the chair and bends down to help her unstrap the boy. Turning to Arcadia, Headmaster opens his mouth, pauses, and then closes it again.

Between them, Arthur looks up. "So how did I do?" he asks. "Was the saliva a bit much? I read that sometimes people wet their pants. I'm all for method acting—but I wasn't prepared to go that far."

"You did fine, Arthur," she replies. "You did fine."

7
PUNISHMENT

"I'm guessing you thought it would take longer than twenty-four hours for the beast to take over?" The other students have shuffled off to classes, but she stays behind to help Mr. Ormiston sweep the floor. The cleaning staff will be returning soon, but she is curious about what led him to support this odd enterprise.

Headmaster pauses for a moment, then nods. "Ah yes, *Lord of the Flies*. It took weeks before those boys killed anyone. I did think the Priory School might last more than a day."

She uses a pan to gather up a pile of cornflakes. "And was there some educational purpose? Or did Sebastian just talk you into it?"

He sighs. "A bit of both. Master Harker was doing an assignment on a prison experiment done back in the 1970s at Stanford University. A professor got some students to pretend to be guards, while others were prisoners."

"I've heard of it," she says. "The guards became sadistic and the experiment was abandoned in less than a week. It was controversial, but supported the theory that people's behaviour depends less on their inherent virtue than on the situation in which they find themselves."

"Yes." Mr. Ormiston crouches to pick up a slice of bread that has landed butter-down on the floor. "Sebastian seemed genuinely interested in the psychology behind it and, for the first time, had done some original thinking about a piece of schoolwork. I told him that I was willing to relax school rules to see how the students behaved in a rule-free environment, but he seems to have taken the Stanford prison experiment as a model instead of a warning."

An interesting explanation, but surely not a sufficient one to divert the entire school. "Of course you weren't just helping him with his assignment," she says. "You were also conducting your own experiment."

He drops the bread in a garbage bag and straightens. "When Sebastian came to me, with Arthur proposing to play the role of victim, I thought it might provide a teachable moment. That our students might see that they have the resilience necessary to remain moral in the face of evil—or that they need it. But what about you? Why didn't you act to stop things earlier?"

"It was evident that we were being tested," she says, "and I presumed that you wanted the experiment to play out rather than be stopped simply because it was artificial.

Sebastian isn't that good an actor. And though Arthur pulled off a very good Hamlet last year, being electrocuted requires perfect timing and his was a little off."

Mr. Ormiston laughs wryly. "I should have known that you would see through it. At some point we are all tested, Arcadia. Even you will be, one day. And when that happens, I hope you're strong enough to realise that doing the right thing doesn't just mean following your brain, but also following your heart."

Most of the floor is now clear of debris. "You had best get on to class," Mr. Ormiston says. "And I'd better go and check on Miss Doran."

From its perch on a windowsill, the sparrow swoops down to pick up a last crust of bread, flying out the open door and into the chill morning air.

———— ∿ɿoᴑᴑɿ ————

"You, the students of the Priory School, come from some of the best families in our land. You want for nothing."

It is evening and Mr. Ormiston now stands in the pulpit at Chapel. Friday evensong is normally optional, but an announcement about the reinstatement of school rules came with a polite encouragement to attend. The chaplain, Mr. Roundhay, beamed as he commenced the service, thinking that additional such debacles might bring more of the students closer to God. After the Bible readings—Proverbs 25: "He that hath no rule over his own spirit is like a city that is broken down, and without walls"—Mr. Ormiston rose to deliver a homily that is less meditation on the scripture than on the weakness of the human heart.

"The school provides a safe environment within which to develop your boundless potential," he continues. "And yet," now his voice deepens, "and yet you so quickly descend into the very worst of what humanity has to offer. Instead of loving your neighbour, you turn on him; instead of protecting the weak, you bay for his pain." He shakes his head. "I blame myself. This was a test for which many of you were not ready. I overestimated the extent to which we have prepared you for the trials of the world."

Mr. Ormiston is being hard on himself. Perhaps he should be. Surveying the young men and women seated before him, he runs a hand through hair that has started to grey. "But there will come a time when you can no longer blame your actions on your genes or on your circumstances. There comes a time at which you must take responsibility. That's what defines the transition to adulthood.

"Immanuel Kant once wrote that you should never treat the humanity in someone—even in yourself—merely as a means to an end. That humanity is an end in itself; it's what *makes* us human. If that message resonates with even some of you, then this whole sorry episode may yet have been worthwhile."

He returns to his seat and Mr. Roundhay leads the final prayer, asking them to open their hymnals to the Old

Hundredth as the recessional. The words were memorised long ago, but she opens the book in solidarity with her peers:

All people that on earth do dwell,
Sing to the Lord with cheerful voice.

Her mouth sings and her eyes are on the page, but the focus of her attention is neither lyrics nor music. It is on the precise handwriting that runs down the side of the hymnal.

Frph dw plgqljkw. Frph dorqh.

She looks around Chapel but all she sees are students and staff. Beside her, Henry's blond hair bobs in time with the music. From the altar, Mr. Roundhay catches her eye and smiles, but it is the genial pastor's smile he gives everyone.

She returns her gaze to the text. A simple Caesar's code, it substitutes each letter with one further down the alphabet. A basic cipher, but sufficient to make a string of letters look superficially random. Take the third letter before each, however, and the text reads:

Come at midnight. Come alone.

After the service, she walks across the quadrangle with Henry. A few stars are visible in the moonless sky, though clouds are beginning to obscure them.

"So," Henry muses, "do you think Harriet really would have electrocuted Arthur?"

"I think the answer to that question is why Harriet is still with the nurse. Peer pressure can bring out the worst in people."

"Not you, eh? You don't do things just because other people want you to."

She shrugs. "It depends who is asking. But peer pressure means doing things just because other people *expect* you to do so. That's rarely a good reason."

They keep walking, their footsteps naturally falling into a single rhythm. She lengthens and slows her gait, Henry unconsciously following her until at last he almost trips.

"What was that all about?" he asks, laughing.

"Trying to find your own rhythm in the world can be tricky. It's often easier to give in to peer pressure."

They approach the dormitory building, though she has no intention of sleeping. Given what she plans to do, an insurance policy is in order.

"Henry," she begins. "You know how you can use your computer to find your phone when you lose it?"

"You never lose your phone, Arcadia."

"OK, but for people who do, you know the feature."

"Yes, I've used it myself," he says. "Once. Maybe three

times. I might even use it again when I buy a new phone to replace the one that Moira fried."

"And you know you can also use it to track someone else's phone also?"

"You mean stalk them?"

"I suppose it could look a bit like that," she replies. "But if, say, someone was going to do something in which there was a moderate amount of risk, it might be nice to know that someone else could find you."

He stops walking. "What exactly are you involved in now, Arcadia?"

"I don't know. Yet. But there's something connecting Moira, Lysander Starr, Miss Alderman—and Dr. Bell."

"The guy from Magdalen?"

"Yes."

"Arcadia, when you start using phrases like 'moderate amount of risk' it means you're going to do something most people would regard as foolhardy. Whatever you're doing, don't try to do it alone?"

"I'm not, Henry. Knowing that you have my back means a lot to me. In any case, I don't think it rises to the level of 'foolhardy'. But if it makes you feel better, here are my login details so that you can find my phone—and me." She passes him a slip of paper, their fingers brushing as he takes it.

"With these I could also buy some movies and see all your photos, right?"

"I wouldn't get your hopes up, Henry."

He folds the paper and puts it into his wallet. "Is this like people swapping apartment keys? Do I need to give you my login details now also when I get a new phone?"

"Don't be silly, Henry," she says. "That's hardly necessary—I know them already."

She retires to her room but does not change. It is almost midnight when she receives a text message. The number is blocked, but the message itself clear enough:

Chapel. Come at once if convenient. If inconvenient, come all the same.

Wrapping a coat around herself, she separates her phone from its charger and puts it into her bag. From the darkened dormitory she slips onto the quadrangle. The night air is crisper than usual, possibly heralding snow. Her footsteps on the grass are the only sound as she crosses the lawn and approaches the darkened Chapel.

Though Mr. Roundhay retires to his own quarters in the evening, the doors to Chapel are never locked. Inside, a dim glow comes from the chancel lamp above the altar. The air is slightly warmer than outside, but she keeps her coat wrapped around her as she moves down the aisle. Nothing stirs.

The altar was stripped of its linen after the service,

but something now stands upon it. Chess pieces? She approaches the sanctuary. A board rests on the altar, complete with wooden chessmen arranged in a late stage endgame. Curious. Up to that point it seemed most likely that the midnight assignation was with Miss Alderman.

"You can come out now, Moira," she says.

There is a chuckle from the vestry and the other her emerges, clad in black once more but with her hair pulled back in a ponytail. In the darkness it is hard to tell, but her hair looks paler. Turning grey? "Shh," Moira raises a finger to her lips. "I'm supposed to be dead." The movements are still erratic, but the other her seems none the worse for wear after faking her own demise. "I can't believe you didn't come to my funeral."

"Was there a funeral?" she, Arcadia, asks.

"You didn't even bury my ashes? What kind of a sister are you?" The outrage appears genuine for a moment, then Moira breaks character and laughs. She takes a swig from a bottle.

"Back on the wagon, I see?"

"I'm refining the patches." The other her gestures at the board. "So, how about a nice game of chess?"

"It looks like you're already in the middle of a game."

"My opponent couldn't stay. Why not see if you can finish it? You play white. Your challenge is to try to checkmate me in six moves."

"Fine," she says, studying the board. Moira's games usually have a point; getting to it sooner might enable her to ask some questions of her own for a change. Then she sees that there is only one legal move for white anyway.

Chess grandmasters plan several moves ahead, though how many depends on the state of the game. As the number of pieces shrink, so do the options. "My king is pinned and all my pawns but one are blocked. All I can do is move the centre pawn."

Moira giggles. "You know the old Stoic saying: 'The Fates lead the willing; the unwilling, they drag.'"

Arcadia moves her pawn to d4 and Moira responds by advancing a piece down the king's knight file to b5. The same constraints mean that for her next move she can still only move the same pawn, now coming to rest at d5 behind another white pawn, blocking it and also threatening stalemate.

Yet Moira also has only one legal move, which is to advance her own pawn down to b4 where it is threatened by Arcadia's.

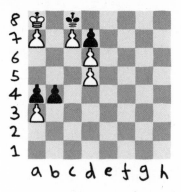

Again there is a single legal move: to take Moira's pawn at b4. And then she sees the inevitability of it—each of them has a passed pawn, each heading down an open file. Moira's will reach the end first, but the following move will see her own pawn queened at b8 even as it checkmates black's king.

The Fates lead the willing; the unwilling, they drag.

Moira sees that she understands and begins packing up the pieces. "Well, wasn't that fun," the other her says briskly, taking another drink from the bottle.

"So you invited me here to play a pointless game of chess in which neither of us had any decisions to make?"

"Hey, before you criticise someone, walk a mile in their shoes. That way, when you do criticise them, you're a mile away—and you have a new pair of shoes." Moira gives an exasperated sigh. "No, I invited you here to have a girl-to-girl chat, maybe do each other's hair and talk about boys."

"For someone who's only two or three years old, you do a pretty good impression of a teenager."

The other her folds up the chessboard. "At last the scales fall from her eyes and she begins to understand the world around her! Yes, big sister, I may have been given the souped up genes, but you'll always have time on me. That second law of thermodynamics is a bitch."

"I'm afraid there's daylight between you and a point, Moira. Are you here tonight to lecture me on the illusion of free will?"

"Hah," the other her laughs. "Quite the opposite. You see I'm normally something of a loner—trouble trusting people due to my atypical upbringing, you know. And right now I'm trying to decide whether to cross this bridge between us—or burn it down. But, as I always tell myself, a mind is like a parachute: it only works when it's open. Though, for what it's worth, you don't actually need a parachute to skydive. You only need one if you want to skydive twice.

"I do confess that I've enjoyed getting to know you—it's sort of like watching myself in slow motion. A flashlight can't shine on itself, you know. The diaries were illuminating, also. I hope you don't mind me reading them. I figured that since we're family and all it would be OK." Another swig from the bottle. "I did like your response to that marshmallow test business. Not bad for a four-year-old. Me, I would have stolen the keys to the cabinet, burned the laboratory to the ground, and toasted the marshmallows in the flames. But that's a pyromaniac for you."

"You're also kind of a sociopath."

Moira freezes for a moment, an unsettling interruption to her fluid movements. "You raise an interesting point. I admit that I'm not exactly a 'people person'. But on the anti-social rollercoaster am I more sociopath or psychopath? Did my petri dish and society make me this way, or was I born like this? Maybe a little bit of both. Or maybe I just enjoy living in the moment. You should try it, Arky—live a little!"

The other her drains the remaining liquid from the bottle, shaking it to get the last drops. Raising a finger, her sister ducks back into the vestry and returns with a backpack.

"Now tell *me* something, Moira," Arcadia says. "Why pretend to kill yourself? And why try to get me arrested for robbing the Tower of London?"

"Isn't it obvious?" Moira replies, opening the backpack

on the altar and putting the chessboard and pieces inside, while rummaging around for something else.

She realises that this is how she must sound to other people, and begins to understand their frustration. "No," she confesses. "It's not."

Moira rolls her eyes and speaks more slowly. "I needed to disappear for a while. And as for you, how else was I meant to protect you?"

"Protect me?"

"Having decided not to kill you myself, it seemed a waste to let someone else harm you. So I decided to keep you safe. Since I couldn't watch you twenty-four hours a day, I thought I would delegate it to Her Majesty's Prison Service."

"But keep me safe from whom?"

Moira has stopped searching in the backpack and her eyes narrow, resting on something over Arcadia's shoulder. "From him."

In the doorway, a man takes off a hat that bears a fine sheen of white. The first snow of the year. Even as he enters the room, the warmth of the air causes its crystalline structure to break down and the frost becomes mere damp.

"You're a difficult one to track, Moira, I'll give you that," Dr. Bell says, stamping his feet to warm up. "Keeping tabs on Miss Arcadia, on the other hand, is child's play. And I knew that eventually you would come for her. Bravo, by the way, on your spectacular immolation. 'Nothing in her life became her like the leaving it.' Or something like that." He continues to walk slowly down the nave. "You almost had me fooled." He slows as he nears the altar. "Almost."

Beside her Moira is looking in the backpack once more, a grunt of frustration escaping her lips.

"What's the matter, Moira?" Dr. Bell inquires. "Looking for something?"

The other her puts the backpack on the altar. "The backdoor to the vestry. You're quieter than I thought."

Dr. Bell smiles, but there is no kindness in it. "Indeed, I found this in your bag while you were playing your little game of chess." He holds up a bottle filled with fluid. "I won't ask who won—I don't want to kindle any sibling rivalry."

"Give me my bottle," Moira says.

Dr. Bell regards the plastic container, tipping it to watch the liquid move. Then he returns his gaze to Moira. "You didn't say the magic word," he taunts.

This seems unwise. In one smooth movement, Moira produces a gun from the rear waistband of her trousers. The same revolver pointed at Arcadia a year earlier.

"Give me my bottle," Moira says, "or I'll shoot you in the head."

"That's more than one word." Dr. Bell tuts.

"Now." Moira cocks the gun.

Will the other her really shoot? Possibly, but a head wound would make answers from Dr. Bell unlikely. "I suggest you do what Moira says," Arcadia offers.

Dr. Bell hesitates for a moment, then throws Moira the bottle.

Keeping the gun steady in her right hand, Moira catches it in her left. "Thanks," the other her says, putting the bottle on the table while the revolver remains trained on Dr. Bell. "So Arky, people like to say that revenge is a dish best served cold, but I tend to think it's best served as a ten-course tasting menu. Did you know, for example, that if you shoot someone in the spleen it can take hours for them to die?"

The barrel now points at Dr. Bell's abdomen.

"I agree that's one way to explore human biology," Arcadia says, "but do you mind if we ask him some questions first? Like how he's connected to Lysander Starr?"

"Oh do catch up, Arky!" Moira exclaims. "Can we really be related?"

And then she sees it: Dr. Bell visiting her in hospital a year earlier. A doctor at a teaching hospital who is also a professor. The professor. Dr. Bell guilty and looking at Arky. Dr. Bell who signed the Hebron's death certificates. "You taught Miss Alderman," she says. "And Lysander Starr. You were the professor who sent Miss Alderman to my school. And then you sent Starr to do some 'housekeeping' and kill us both."

"Ah Lysander." Dr. Bell is close to them now. "A brilliant young man, but never the sharpest pencil in the box. He misunderstood what I meant by 'housekeeping'.

He had overstepped and risked compromising our whole enterprise, just as Milton had. And so I had to take action to remove him."

"*You* blew up his car?"

"With a little help from Moira here, who had given me the explosives. I like to think of myself as somewhat enterprising, but it's dashed difficult to acquire significant quantities of C4 on the open market."

"I can introduce you to my guy, if you like," Moira says. "A nice ex-SAS chap. You'd like him."

"I'm sure I would."

How has she not realised Dr. Bell's connection? And then she sees that she did: a hazy memory of him visiting her in hospital a year earlier; more recently her own withholding of the information that Moira was alive when he came to the police station. At the time, she thought she could not trust herself.

"Why are you here, why now?" she asks.

"I came to try to talk some sense into Moira. That this petty vendetta must end and that I can help her lead a normal life."

"Back to your petri dish?" Moira scoffs. "I don't think so. In any case, I don't want 'normality'. I want to shine. But first I want to engage in a bit of Oedipal rage."

Once again the barrel points at Dr. Bell's abdomen.

"Moira," she says. "Why didn't you just warn me? I was standing there with Dr. Bell at Magdalen and you threw a Molotov cocktail at us both. You could have just told me, rather than hiding a jewel in my desk and phoning the cops."

"Yes, well the simple things in life are kind of boring, aren't they?" Moira responds. "And when you started palling around with the good doctor here, I had to be sure you simply were that gullible and not in cahoots with him." Gun still trained on Dr. Bell, the other her pops open the top of the second bottle and swigs a mouthful.

"And you." Arcadia turns to Dr. Bell. "Why get me to come to Magdalen? You wanted to keep an eye on your placebo, keep me in a controlled environment only slightly larger than the laboratory in which you imprisoned Moira?"

"Placebo?" Dr. Bell cannot suppress a laugh. "Oh my dear girl, you really do understand nothing. What on earth did Lysander tell you?"

"He said you were editing DNA in order to bypass evolution. That Moira was the future, and I was the past."

Again, he laughs. How has she not noticed the meanness in him before? "Close, but no cigar," he says. "But there will be time in due course to explain."

From the corner of her eye, she sees the gun barrel wobble.

"So stupid," Moira is saying, contempt in her voice but her precise articulation is breaking down. "Arky, take the gun. Shoot him. So obvious." The gun drops onto the altar as Moira stumbles. "Flunitrazepam in the electrolytes.

Shoot him, Arky, or we're both dead." The other her leans against the altar, knees collapsing.

"What have you done to her?" Arcadia demands.

"As she correctly diagnosed, I added a little something to her go-go juice," he replies, taking a long piece of wood out of his coat pocket. "A trick I learned from you, Moira. 'Roofies', I believe the kids call them today. Just something to make it a little easier to bring you both in without a fight."

Moira sinks below the altar, murmuring on the descent into unconsciousness.

"And yet I didn't drink anything," Arcadia says, leaning over to pick up the revolver. "That was your mistake."

As she turns back to face him she feels a prick in her neck. The piece of wood is now at his lips. A blowpipe? A burning sensation starts to spread through her body.

"Which is why I brought this," Dr. Bell holds up the small weapon in his hands. "The first time I went to Thailand to collect rhesus monkeys, the locals used blowpipes like this one. Today we have tranquiliser guns, but I still prefer to do it old school every now and then."

The burning is making it hard to breathe. Her hand closes around the handle of the gun but lacks the strength to pick it up. A fog comes over her. What does she want the gun for again?

"The poison is fast-acting, I'm told, and quite disorienting."

Why does her tongue feel so big? Oh if only she could

get a nice block of ice. Her skin is so itchy. Ooh, ice would be nice. Who is speaking?

"You might want to sit down, because when it reaches the brain the—"

Darkness.

8
CAPTIVE

A low hum. Ventilation? And the faint buzz of many fluorescent lights. Also a clock. How long has she been unconscious? Impossible to tell until she can see again. The left side of her face is cold, resting on something hard.

She has been knocked out before, but the poison dart is cruder than a tranquiliser gun. Her muscles ache and a throbbing clouds her head. Focus on the senses that work.

Breathing. Someone nearby inhales and exhales with the regular rhythm of sleep. A snore escapes his lips. Or hers.

She focuses on her own respiration, taking air in through her nose. She almost gags at the smell. The reek of bodily waste permeates the air, leavened by an earthiness. Not a sewer—an overflowing toilet?

She is indoors, a temperature-controlled environment with fluorescent lights. Dr. Bell said he was going to bring her and Moira somewhere. Is this what Moira called her petri dish?

With what feels like a heroic effort, she pushes her eyelids up. The brightness of the room is blinding as she focuses on the figure next to her. Horizontal lines separate them, but the image slowly resolves. Too small to be Moira, is it a child? He or she shifts in sleep, lips smacking softly. A baby? It is wrapped in a shaggy blanket, or wearing some kind of rough woollen clothing.

Again, the stench of faeces is overpowering. It does serve to clear her vision, however, and she looks once more at the pink face. What sort of baby has facial hair? She shakes her head, a movement large enough to attract her neighbour's attention. The yellow eyes open—yellow?—pupils constricting even as they focus on her own. Bared teeth and a screech shock her into wakefulness as she and the monkey in the next cage stare at each other.

"You're awake then." Her own voice, Moira's voice, somewhere nearby.

"Where are you?" she says, coughing to clear the phlegm that has built up in her throat. "Where are we?"

"The first question is easy: I'm about two metres away from you. If the poison used on you was the juice from the giant taro, your vision should be returning soon and you'll see me. If, on the other hand, it was from the seeds of the strychnine tree then—well, then you would already be dead."

She pulls herself up onto her elbows, the monkey—a rhesus macaque, by the look of it—watching her carefully. It has light brown fur with a tuft of white on its forehead.

The cage is big enough for her to sit but not stand. There is no sign of her bag.

"The second question," Moira continues, "is more challenging. From the state of my bladder, I would estimate that I was unconscious for about six hours. A roofie wouldn't have knocked me out that long, so the good doctor must have administered some kind of tranquiliser to keep me under. It is possible that we were travelling all that time—but unlikely. More probable is that we are somewhere near Oxford. My best guess is a warehouse in an industrial estate on the edge of town. Given our proximity to a river and its size, I would think we're on the bank of the Thames, which for reasons of tradition and pretension is here called the Isis."

For the first time, she notices the sound of rushing water. She blinks and registers the blurry outline of Moira in a cage opposite her. Craning her neck she looks down the corridor formed by barred metal doors. At least two rows of ten cages, though she cannot see how many are occupied. Above them, fluorescent tubes illuminate the room in a pale light.

"Why are we here?"

"You're just full of questions today, aren't you, Arky? How about you use some of your own little grey cells for a change? Why do you think we're here?"

Another shake of her head merely causes the fog in her brain to swirl. She closes her eyes and breathes slowly, pulling her thoughts into line. "Dr. Bell is the professor who sent Miss Alderman to the Priory School, keeping an eye on my part of the experiment about the same time that you were escaping from yours. He's been using gene-editing technology on human embryos—on you. But he started with monkeys first? And he's brought us here because we know too much."

"Hmm. OK, maybe I'll give you another gentleman's pass for that. You're on the right track, but heading in the wrong direction. If we simply knew too much then he would have used the strychnine on you and any number of poisons on me." Moira takes a drink from a plastic bottle, her electrolytic cocktail. Dr. Bell must want them both alive and functional.

"Right, right." She sits up properly. At one end of the row of cages is a wooden door with a glass panel; at the other are two padded chairs with restraints. They remind her of Sebastian's "old sparky", but these have elaborate helmets. Too big for the monkeys, they are designed for humans.

"We're still useful to him. He needs something from us, more data for his experiment? Or is there some sentimental reason why he hasn't killed us?"

The door opens and Dr. Bell walks in. "To be honest, it's a little of both," he says. He has been listening from an adjoining room. The door was only open for a moment, but her bag is on the floor of that room. "I do apologise for the simple accommodations and the manner in which you were brought here, but it was necessary."

Her phone is inside the bag. She has left it switched on, which means that Henry can locate it. She needs to distract Dr. Bell long enough that Henry will realise she is missing and try to find her.

"Why was it necessary?" she asks.

Dr. Bell walks down the corridor, inspecting each cage. He is holding a tray with a plate and two drink containers. "Moira, here, was bent on interfering and had to be stopped. As for you, it was quickly becoming clear that the relationship of trust that I had so carefully cultivated was beginning to break down."

Keep him talking. "Why would you say that?"

As he approaches, the monkey in the cage next to her bares its teeth and hisses. If its earlier screech upon seeing her was fear, this is closer to anger. He does not seem to notice. "I would like to attribute it to my uncanny ability to read emotions," he says. "But in fact it was because I know that the woman you call Miss Alderman has contacted you."

There is no natural light, but if six hours have passed it should be dawn. How long before Henry notices that she is missing?

"By the way." Dr. Bell is still talking. "I must apologise that while bringing you here I dropped your phone." He places the tray on a bench next to the cages and picks up what is left of her device. The screen is shattered and it has been snapped almost in half. "Well, that's not quite true. In fact, I dropped it, stepped on it a few times, and finally reversed over it with my van. I am so terribly sorry."

He puts the phone back on the tray and gestures to the plate, on which there are two croissants. "We did have a somewhat nicer facility, but dear Moira rather spoiled that when she blew it up. The least hospitality I can offer you, however, is a simple breakfast. There's a lovely café down the street that does pastries and a decent coffee. A skinny flat white for you, Arcadia, and a triple espresso for you, Moira."

Neither she nor Moira reach for the gifts, as it is clear that there will be conditions.

"But it doesn't seem right just to *give* them to you," he says. "It is a Saturday morning, after all, Arcadia. How about we start it with a nice puzzle? Perhaps a matchstick problem, just for old time's sake?"

Locked in a cage solving quizzes for food. Is he pushing the lab rat metaphor a little far? She contemplates saying this out loud, but antagonising her captor seems unlikely to help at this point. How did she fail to see this side of him?

"Now Moira," he turns to the other her, raising a finger. "No helping. If you tell her the answer then there will be no breakfast for either of you." From his pocket, he takes out a box of matches and begins arranging them on the tray. Roman numerals again, but a more complicated equation.

From her cage, Moira glances at it for a moment and

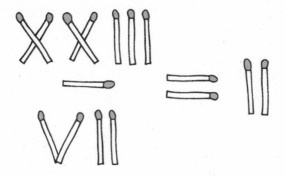

then laughs. "Just as well—it's an easy one. I like my coffee warm. Come on then, Arky. Shake a leg."

Moira might be accustomed to being poked and prodded in this way, yet the other her's confidence is oddly unsettling. On the puzzle itself, Moira might have seen it before—or maybe is just that quick. Despite the absurdity of the situation, she tries to concentrate. Push everything out of her mind except the problem to be solved. Twenty-three divided by seven equals two. Her mind begins to clear. No, it doesn't. It equals 3.285714... but Roman numerals are ill-equipped to handle decimals.

Dr. Bell positions the tray next to the barred door of her cage. From the adjacent cell, the macaque with the white tuft looks on, baring its teeth at their captor when he approaches but relaxing when he steps back.

In such puzzles, the aim is to move the fewest matchsticks to leave a valid equation. Removing two of the vertical matches from XXIII leaves XXI; placing one of those on the right hand side transforms II to III—

twenty-one divided by seven equals three, but there is a leftover match.

A single matchstick from either side could be placed over the equals sign, rendering the non-equation correct but pointless. Unlikely to be the answer.

"Do hurry up, Arky. My espresso is getting cold."

She ignores the other her. Roman numerals are cumbersome to use for even basic arithmetic; little wonder they were overtaken by the Arabic version used today. The influence of Rome does live on, of course, in the Latin alphabet. Curious that Ancient Greece, which laid the foundation of Western politics, philosophy, and culture, is barely visible on a modern keyboard—with the exception of the humble letter "Y", which the French still call the "*i grec*". The influence of Greek mathematicians like Pythagoras does live on, partly through the use of Greek letters for certain concepts such as…

She takes one of the vertical matches from the

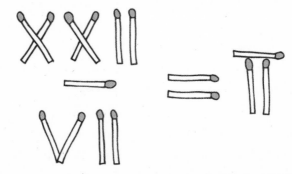

numerator and lays it across the top of the two matchsticks on the right-hand side.

"It should really be *approximately* equals," she says. "But twenty-two divided by seven equals 3.142857… which is tolerably close to 3.141592… Or, more precisely, π—*pi*."

"Oh good show, Miss Arcadia," Dr. Bell seems genuinely pleased. He places a croissant and a coffee in the metal hatch outside each cage and slides it in. The design makes it possible to do this without risk of them touching him.

"Word for the wise, Arky," Moira observes. "Don't bite the hand that feeds you. Grab it, steal the keys, and make a run for it. Isn't that right, doc?"

Dr. Bell rubs his own hand, an old injury? "Quite, Moira. Enjoy your breakfast, ladies. I have some errands to run but will be back within the hour."

Seeing Moira drink her espresso, she eats her own croissant and tastes the coffee. Very good indeed. The caffeine also helps to make her more alert. Why would Dr. Bell want that?

"I guess you should have stayed in Paris," she says, breaking off a piece of pastry to share it with the macaque.

"What?" Moira takes a bite of her own croissant and then laughs. "Oh, the escape room. No, though I did learn French one weekend, I've not yet been to the city of light.

Do you know how often they change their underwear?" She pauses, then adds: "*C'est pas quotidian, hein?*"

"But you said—"

"I say a lot of things," Moira cuts her off. "And I say them for a reason, but that's not the same as them necessarily being true." The other her raises an eyebrow slightly

A signal? Clearly Dr. Bell can listen to their conversation. Is Moira proposing some kind of plan?

"It's like the riddle about the raven and the writing desk," the other her says. "You did understand it in the end?"

"That some riddles have no answer—or many answers," she replies.

"Precisely. Much like our predicament this morning. There may be no escape, or many. As you will have noticed, the cage doors have electromagnetic locks. There are at least three ways to open them. One is with the key that our friend Dr. Bell carries in his right trouser pocket. A second is with the master switch in the control room at the end of the hall."

"Or else cut power to the whole building," she adds.

"Why, aren't you coming along!" Moira beams at her. "There's probably a backup generator to stop that happening, but yes, it would work."

She tries to ignore the patronising tone.

"But then what?" Moira continues. "Leave this room and where do we go? The good doctor has my revolver and is a passable shot. Perhaps you are familiar with the story of the two hikers in Yosemite National Park who encounter a grizzly bear. One of the men takes off his backpack and starts changing from his hiking shoes into his running shoes. 'What are you doing?' the other man says. 'You can't outrun a grizzly!' The first man looks at his companion: 'But I don't need to outrun the grizzly. I only need to outrun *you*.'"

"So your plan is to outrun me in case Dr. Bell takes a shot at us?"

"Oh my little bag of hammers, you're far too literal. What I mean is that we need a plan that incapacitates the grizzly also. Now let me tell you another story, one I hope you will remember as it may come in handy one day. An Arab sheikh wants to decide which of his two sons should inherit his fortune. There are many versions of this story, but it's always the boys that get the money, for some reason. In any case, the sheikh has an odd challenge: the two boys must race their camels to a distant city, but the one whose camel gets there *last* wins. The two lads wander around aimlessly for days, but neither wants to lose their inheritance by arriving first. Finally, they chance upon a wise man and ask him for guidance. After hearing what he has to say, they jump on the camels and race to the city as fast as they can. So the question is: what did the wise man say to them?"

Another puzzle? Even trapped in a laboratory surrounded by monkeys, Moira seems incapable of having a direct conversation. Was this how she experienced the world from her petri dish—one puzzle at a time?

This one is simpler, however. "He said: 'switch camels'," she replies.

"Exactly." Moira leans back with a satisfied smile and drains the rest of her triple espresso, as if that explained everything.

Arcadia turns to the macaque with the tuft of white hair in the cage next to her own. "Do you understand what my sister is talking about?" she asks, passing the last piece of croissant through the bars of the cage.

It was a rhetorical question, but the monkey looks her in the eye as she speaks. Putting the pastry in its mouth, it raises its shoulders in a gesture that could easily be mistaken for a shrug.

"I need to go to the bathroom," Moira calls out.

"I thought he said he was leaving to run errands," she says.

"Nonsense, he's in the control room or somewhere nearby preparing for whatever is going to happen next."

"Quite right, Moira," Dr. Bell says, walking back in. "And it's soon enough that I don't think a walk to the bathroom is a particularly good idea. You can urinate through the cage floor like the other primates."

"But what if it's a number two?" Moira enquires

innocently. "Do the monkeys throw their faeces at you?"

"They have learned"—he coughs—"not to do so."

"So what does happen next?" Arcadia asks.

Dr. Bell now holds an iPad and is making a show of being absorbed by what it displays. "Next," he says, "we complete your destiny."

"*My* destiny?" she replies. "I thought I was the control, while Moira was the main event."

He chuckles as he looks up from the tablet. "Moira is brilliant in her own way. But when you light a candle with a blowtorch, it tends to burn out too quickly—doesn't it, Moira?"

The other her rolls her eyes.

"Moira is indeed the future," Dr. Bell continues, speaking to Arcadia. "A future in which we can remove genes that bring disease and suffering. But also add genes that will make us smarter, faster, happier. More than that, she is living proof that the brain can develop well after birth. Genes are the source code of life, but epigenetics lets us adapt that programme—adding neurons, repairing connections. We can enhance the brain well beyond what we might now call genius. She told you, I presume, about her IQ tests?" A sideways glance at Moira gets another eye roll.

"Unfortunately," he says, "the same biological processes that accelerated her neurological development accelerated everything else also. You have doubtless worked out her age is far less than her physiology suggests." He turns back to Moira. "We'll be celebrating your fourth birthday soon, won't we?"

"That's twenty-eight in dog years," the other her replies with a wink. In the fluorescent light, the grey in Moira's hair is now more evident.

"As we refine the technique, there are some things we can adapt, of course." Though still fiddling with the iPad, he is watching Arcadia carefully now. "Repairing severely damaged brains—a patient suffering from cerebral hypoxia, for example. Lack of oxygen can drive the brain into a coma, but the treatment I have developed could reverse neuronal cell death and bring about a partial or even full recovery for such a patient."

For such a patient as Mother.

"So why haven't you published this research, started clinical trials?" She has read every medical journal article on comas published in the last thirty years; there has been no mention of this treatment. Even as the words leave her mouth, it is clear that she is being manipulated. But she has vowed to try.

"This technology is not yet mainstream, shall we say." Dr. Bell flicks at the iPad with a frown, dismissing a piece of unhelpful information. "So-called 'ethics' can be a great hindrance to great work. That's why my research on rhesus monkeys had to go underground, so to speak. Between the government and the damned animal liberationists it was becoming harder and harder to run a laboratory. As for clinical trials, the human subject protocols at Oxford would have made my work impossible. Even if I did receive approval, how does one demonstrate the upper limits of intellectual capacity when the volunteers are likely to be the dregs of society—the unemployed and ex-prisoners? The macaques I could import through the black market, but where was I going to get human subjects whom I could groom for greatness?"

"I thought university students participated in those studies all the time," she says.

"They do, but I needed a controlled environment from before birth. To measure the impact of parentage and genetic enhancements against environmental factors like school and home life—nature vs nurture—with an eye to the next phase of human evolution. Yes, Moira may be the future. But you, Miss Arcadia, *you* are very much the present."

"Why me? When the Hebrons died, you signed their death certificates and put me with Mother and Father. You arranged for me to go to the Priory School under Milton and sent Miss Alderman to keep an eye on us both. But why did you choose me in the first place?"

"I didn't really choose you, Miss Arcadia. We chose each other."

She shakes her head, a truth dawning that she is unwilling to accept. "What are you talking about?"

"Here it comes," says Moira. "You can choose your friends but you sho' can't choose your family."

Dr. Bell puts the iPad on the bench and approaches her cage. "It means that you're my daughter, Arcadia."

9
IDENTITY

"That's impossible," she says, even as she realises that it is not. "You said your wife died years before I was born." Yet he also said that she reminds him of her.

Dr. Bell stands before her cage door, examining her closely. "CRISPR technology may be new, but frozen embryo transfer is a technique from the previous century. My wife died in childbirth, the birth of our son, but we had taken the precaution of freezing embryos to carry on our work."

"You experimented on your own children?"

"We experimented on *ourselves*," he says firmly. "And look what we achieved. Edith and I were among the brightest of our generation, but all we could do to expand our own horizons was to use nootropics as stimulants. The quantum leap was the generation gap: taking the best of ourselves and then supplementing those genes with the best possible environment from the moment of conception.

"It's not so unusual, I suppose. Many women today take fish oil, folic acid, vitamin supplements, and so on during pregnancy. Edith and I developed a more elaborate regime of fatty amine compounds to encourage neurological development. There were some side effects in the early stages. Our son was born with a metabolic disorder—but, of course, you know all about that."

Magnus. "Your wife died when Magnus was born?"

"Yes. He was an enormous baby but she insisted on carrying him to term. When he was at last delivered the strain was too much for her—she suffered a postpartum haemorrhage and— and died. I vowed to carry on our work and, seven years later, you were born."

"And you, you just gave us up without wanting to be part of our lives?"

"I gave you up so that I could help shape your life better than a mere parent ever could! I couldn't be a father and a scientist. So I found a couple who wanted children and were willing to accept the conditions that came with it: diet, tests, a school environment all geared towards enhancing your abilities."

"*Mens sana in corpore sano*," she whispers. Then more loudly: "But to what end?"

"Why does there need to be an end? Isn't the pursuit of knowledge for its own sake what has always driven innovation?"

Necessity also typically plays a role, but hold that thought for later. "And then you wanted to go further," she says, "beyond what was possible in nature, so you created Moira."

"Only one of the original frozen embryos was viable—you—so as a further safeguard I caused it to divide and re-divide, keeping the monozygotes stored in liquid nitrogen. It took another decade before the technology was available to move beyond nurturing the strongest qualities in one embryo to editing the very genes of another. The risks increased also, but as a prototype Moira is truly remarkable."

"A prototype?"

"I suppose she wasn't technically the first," Dr. Bell replies. "After you, Arcadia, came Beatrix, then Cassiopeia, Delilah, and so on. But none of them survived more than a couple of days. Lyra lasted almost a week, but it was only with Moira that we achieved stability. Though I'm not sure a psychologist would entirely agree that you are stable, eh Moira?"

The other her leans back in her cage, fingers interlaced behind her head. "Oh I'm crazy like a fox, *Daddy*. Remember, Arky: if you're going through hell, keep going."

"Wait." She processes information faster than most, but this is a lot, even for her. "I have—I had—eleven other sisters, all of whom died because you were experimenting on them?"

"You make it sound very dramatic," says her fath— says Dr. Bell with a frown. "They were clones and they died well before they had the capacity for conscious thought.

We only even gave them all names because Moira insisted. 'Thirteen' wasn't good enough for her poetry, apparently."

"That's not the point," Arcadia interjects.

"Of course it's the point! Through Moira, we have demonstrated our ability to change our very genetic makeup and radically expand our intellectual potential. The next step is to ensure that that potential lasts over a full life cycle or longer."

"What's that supposed to mean? Even if Moira is only a few years old, if you could accelerate her growth surely you can slow it down again?"

"Alas, no," he replies. "The acceleration is at the genetic level and this affects cell growth and decay through her entire body. You know what telomeres are, I assume?"

She does. Stretches of DNA at the ends of chromosomes, they are sometimes compared to plastic tips on shoelaces. Telomeres help prevent the chromosomes from fraying, which would scramble genetic information. Over time, however, they shorten and eventually cannot hold the chromosome together. Linked with ageing, the shoelace analogy is sometimes replaced with the metaphor of a bomb fuse. "You light a candle with a blowtorch and it burns out too quickly," she whispers.

"That's right, Arky," Moira pipes up cheerily. "I'm dying. Well, technically we're all dying. But I'm likely to die first, right, doc? That is, unless you want to hand me back my revolver so that I can push you to the front of the queue."

"Not today, Moira," is his deadpan response.

"I'm sorry," she says to her sister.

"Don't be," Moira replies. "Life's a terminal disease for everyone, Arky. I've probably got another few years. And though Dr. Feelgood here has given up on me, I have a few ideas that I want to try out before shuffling off this mortal coil."

"I haven't given up on you, Moira," Dr. Bell says. "Just this version of you. That's why *you're* here—to help fine-tune mark fourteen. I'm thinking Natalia might be a nice name?"

"How about 'No Man'?" the other her replies.

"Hmm?" Dr. Bell frowns again. "Now you're confusing your Greek myths. That's Odysseus rather than Oedipus."

"Exactly," Moira says, her voice rising, "just before Odysseus puts a red hot poker in his captor's eye!" From within her cage, Moira lunges forward at the bars.

It is a feint, but their captor jumps back despite himself, almost dropping the iPad. As he straightens up, he comes too close to the cage of the white-tufted macaque. With a screech it reaches out a paw and scratches at his face. A line of red appears on his cheek and he winces in pain.

"Nice one, George," Moira says to the monkey, which bares its teeth at Dr. Bell.

"To think," Dr. Bell says, staunching the flow of blood with a handkerchief, "that I was about to say that I would miss you, Moira. I certainly won't be missing *you*," he adds to the macaque, which hisses in response.

Not one sister but a dozen sisters. Their lives created and destroyed by this man. This monster. Her father.

"But why do all this," she says helplessly. "What end could possibly be worth the death of your own children? How smart do I have to be—how smart does Moira, or Natalia, or anyone else have to be to justify all this suffering?"

"Don't be so short-sighted," he replies, examining the reddened handkerchief. "Our intellect is merely the means to an end. The end itself is to fix the ultimate design flaw in humanity."

"Which is our ignorance?"

"No, our death. I am going to cure death." Blood is still flowing from his cheek, undermining the portentous tone of his voice.

"It looks like you might need to cure that cut first," Moira suggests.

Dr. Bell says nothing, turning on his heel to leave the room once more.

"I'm developing a new theory," Moira observes calmly, "about the nature of reality. I've concluded that it's more likely than not that all of this"—she gestures at the cage, the corridor beyond, the lights—"is, in fact, a computer simulation, part of an elaborate video game."

Dr. Bell has been gone for a few minutes, presumably

dressing his wound. Is this some coping mechanism that her sister is developing, to deny the peril they face? "You mean at the end of this we wake up and it's all been a dream?"

"No, I mean that the dream is all there is. It's an ancient idea. The Chinese philosopher Chuang Tzu famously dreamed he was a butterfly, but on waking up struggled to work out if he was Chuang Tzu who had dreamed he was a butterfly—or a butterfly now dreaming that it was Chuang Tzu."

Moira taps the bottom of her coffee to drain the last of the espresso. "Two thousand years ago, that was a nice thought experiment. Today, look at how quickly video games have moved from parallel lines knocking a circle back and forth across a screen, to augmented reality games that involve millions of people simultaneously chasing after Japanese mutant pets. If we assume any kind of continued improvement, eventually virtual reality will be indistinguishable from reality itself. And once that happens, you're down the rabbit hole."

"It sounds like you've watched *The Matrix* a few times too many," she replies. Surely they should spend what energy they have trying to escape the madman who holds them captive.

"With my lifespan, I tend not to watch full-length movies more than once," Moira says, now ripping the paper cup apart to lick the remaining traces of coffee. "I don't mean that we're imprisoned in the game—just that we can't *know* whether we are in it or not. So if it is inevitable that virtual reality is going to reach that point, it starts to become more likely than not that what we think is real is actually a simulation."

She has finished her own coffee and sets the cup down beside her, shifting her legs slightly as they are beginning to go numb from sitting for so long. "Why would anyone spend time and energy making such a pointless game, with such boring outcomes for the vast majority of people?"

"Maybe not everyone's playing. Maybe it's just *you*." Moira pauses, ominously: "Maybe everyone else is *watching* the game, to see if you can work that out." The other her looks up at the ceiling, where a small camera is observing them. "Good morning!" she calls out. "And in case I don't see ya, good afternoon, good evening, and good night!" Discarding the coffee cup, her sister takes another swig of electrolytes and leans back against the wall of her cage. "Or maybe I'm just blowing smoke."

They sit quietly for a full minute, the rushing water of the river and an occasional murmur from one of the macaques the only sound.

"I am sorry that you're dying," she says at last.

"There's nothing to apologise for," Moira responds. "You come from nothing; you're going back to nothing. What have you lost? Nothing! I live life faster than most, anyway. At my back I always hear time's wingèd chariot, hurrying near, and all that." Moira stretches her arms. "Whatever you do, don't call me brave. Why is it that people think that the terminally ill are more noble than everyone else? Surely we've got more of a reason to be more callow, more craven, more angry at the world than those with time on their side."

The other her examines her fingernails absently. "You know, Arky, that's one thing I do like about your brother. He has the right attitude: life is uncertain—start with dessert. What's the point of ploughing through your vegetables in the hope of getting to the pudding when you might choke on a carrot stick? *I* always eat dessert first."

The sound of the wooden door opening alerts them to the return of Dr. Bell. A sticking plaster has been hastily applied to his cheek and he strives to appear unflustered. "Now," he says briskly. "Where were we?"

"Arky's destiny, you curing death, yada yada yada," Moira offers with a yawn.

Dr. Bell chooses to overlook the sarcasm.

"If you're looking at how to prolong life," she says. "Why not start with Moira? Save her, give her a few more years in the sun."

Still fussing with his iPad, Dr. Bell shakes his head. "You suffer from the same limited imagination as everyone else. It's not a question of prolonging life but removing death. People invest billions in ageing, but they focus on the body. Eat well, exercise, tighten the skin, lower the cholesterol, replace an organ here and there. With billions more investment, we might be able to extend life to a hundred and twenty, maybe even a hundred and fifty years. But what sort of life? It all ends the same way: decay. Entropy takes over. Ashes to ashes."

"Funk to funky," Moira adds drily. "We know Major Tom's a junkie."

"Oh very droll, Moira," Dr. Bell says wanly. "The bottom line is that the body, that biology itself, is finite. A tortoise might live for two hundred years, but that's about it for organisms more complex than a jellyfish. The design flaw is with evolution itself. Evolution rewards those who live long enough to pass on their genes—what happens after that is irrelevant.

"But what is a person, anyway. Their body? When someone dies, that's what we deal with. We bury it, we burn it, we leave it out on a rooftop for vultures to consume. Yet it's not what we miss. It's the *mind* that we mourn. Human religions seek out ways for the soul to live beyond the body, returning to earth through reincarnation or ascending to a heavenly paradise."

"In your case, I wouldn't exclude some red hot pokers waiting down in the fiery pits of hell," the other her says airily.

"You of all people should know better than to lecture about theology," Dr. Bell snaps. "Science was held back by religion for centuries because of a fear of knowledge. Adam was right to eat the apple and Eve was right to give it to him."

"That would make you the snake, then?" Moira inquires archly.

"A role I would happily embrace!" Dr. Bell says adamantly. "To liberate humanity from the shackles of our ignorance. But people forget that there were two trees in the Garden of Eden. One was the tree of the knowledge of good and evil. The other was the tree of life. Today I'm more interested in the second of those."

"It's also possible," Moira observes, "that there were no trees at all and the whole story is based on a bad Latin pun: that *mālum*, or 'apple', rhymes with *malum*, meaning 'evil'."

"So what if there was a way for the mind to outlive the body?" Dr. Bell continues, ignoring Moira. "Because information, information doesn't die. And what is the mind, at root? Information. Electrical impulses racing around a neural network. People used to think that consciousness required some divine spark to give it meaning, but now we know that it just arises from the way in which billions of neurons communicate with one another. Like the music on an old vinyl record, it gets scratched the more you play it. Copy it onto a digital format, however, and it can be kept intact forever."

"You want to upload yourself into a computer?" More pieces of the jigsaw fit themselves into place. "That's why you broke into Magnus's work," she says to Moira. "And you," she turns back to Dr. Bell, "you are X?"

"Ironic, isn't it"—he smiles again without mirth—"how helpful your brother has been since he joined my research team. The ravens come home to roost, so to speak." He looks at them expectantly, perhaps hoping for laughter. "No? Oh I thought that was rather good, myself. I do wonder if Magnus will be disappointed, though, when he finds out that I chose you to play the starring role, instead of him?"

"But he told me about Project Raven," she says. "We're a decade from being able to create a computer as complex as the human brain."

"It may be considerably longer than that. But the path is already set. So many people fret about climate change and nuclear war—it's the wrong set of problems. Humans won't become extinct, like the dinosaur and the dodo. With the rise of computers and artificial intelligence, we will simply become obsolete.

"Think about it. The world is already dominated by information. What we experience online is often more 'real' than any fact we bother to check. People talk about the Internet of Things, with more and more devices being connected. Again, they miss the point: soon there will no longer be things *separate* from the Internet."

"But our experience of the world is much more than just the rattling of electrons in our heads," she says. "It's our relationship with others, our connection to that world. Our hormones. You might be able to take a digital picture of neural activity and even model it, but that's not the same as it being alive, as having feelings."

"Nonsense. More than a hundred years ago Thomas Huxley showed that what we think of as conscious feelings are just by-products of physical processes. We convince ourselves that pain makes us wince, that the appearance of a loved one makes us smile. But actually the facial expressions precede our so-called feelings. What we call consciousness is just the steam-whistle on a locomotive: it might be caused by the engine within, but it has no impact on the train itself."

It is a strange metaphor, but she pursues it. "And yet even if all that's true—that we're all just trains pootling along, tooting our whistles—those whistles still have an impact on all the other trains."

"As I said, it was a nineteenth century view of consciousness. In a decade or two, maybe three, the biological notion of existence will go the way of the steam train: a quaint reminder of an inefficient past."

"So what's your rush now?"

"I fear that my own body is starting to give in," he says wearily. "I take care of myself, of course, but statistics are against me avoiding heart disease, dementia, and so on for another ten years. My body is unlikely to last for thirty more." Then force returns to his voice: "I, for one, don't plan on leaving the world just because a set of chemical reactions has run its course."

"You said yourself that we don't yet have computers sophisticated enough to carry all the information from a brain. Project Raven is close to being able to copy the brain but there's nowhere to store that much data."

"Ah Magnus." Dr. Bell shakes his head. "So brilliant

and yet so lazy. Always looking for the simplest solution to the problem, instead of the more arduous task of looking for a simpler problem. That's where you come in."

"Me?" she asks warily.

"Isn't that why parents have children in the first place, to seek a kind of immortality?"

"What are you talking about?"

"We should really have some dramatic music," Moira interjects, leaning forward against her cage door. "Elevate the tension and so on."

"I'm saying," Dr. Bell replies, "that Magnus has ignored the answer that stares him in the face every day. If you can copy the brain, you don't need a machine on which to store it. You just need another brain, preferably a genetically compatible brain—that of your daughter, for example."

10
CRISIS

"You're going to put your mind into my body? That's insane."

"Madness is indeed a possible outcome," Moira observes thoughtfully from her cage. "Whole brain emulation typically assumes putting a copy of the brain onto a blank medium. Writing over an existing mind runs the risk of corruption of data and loss of identity."

"You knew about this?" She turns to her sister, but her movements are sluggish, the numbness in her legs having spread through her body.

Moira returns her gaze. "Not at first. But remember that I did try to protect you from this battle."

"By framing me for theft."

"For the Crown Jewels—you would have been famous!"

Dr. Bell claps his hands together. "Well," he says, "this is all *very* entertaining, but I suppose I had best get on with the procedure. The muscle relaxant in your coffee should have taken effect by now." He takes a key from his pocket and unlocks her cage door.

"Are you sure you don't want to try writing yourself onto my brain, doc?" Moira calls out. "There's room enough here for both of us."

"No thank you, Moira," he replies, pocketing his key. "Once Natalia—or perhaps Octavia or Portia—has achieved stability then a brain such as yours would indeed be an upgrade. Yet I suspect it would need to be wiped clean prior to emulation to avoid my consciousness being overwhelmed by yours."

"Coward," Moira mutters. He ignores her and swings the cage door open.

Arcadia tries to stand but only succeeds in falling into Dr. Bell's arms. "It's a curious feeling, I know," he says, holding her under the armpits as her legs drag on the ground. "Your mind is clear, but your body is unable to respond. For the process to work I need you to be conscious." His breath coming in short gasps, he half-carries her down the row of cages towards the padded chairs. Moira and a line of macaques look on.

"From the tests that I've done," he adds, putting her in one chair and fastening the restraints, "I gather the process is somewhat distressing and quite painful. But at least it should be relatively brief." He lifts the helmet and begins attaching small metal discs connected to cords within it to different parts of her skull.

Despite herself, she finds the process fascinating.

"It's like an EEG?"

He pauses. "More like a reverse electroencephalogram," he says, placing the last electrode and standing back to admire his work. "The device reads my brain activity and then in real time emulates that activity in your brain by forcing a similar pattern on your neural network. When complete, it is I who will be looking out of your eyes." He sits down in the second chair and begins attaching electrodes to his own head.

"And will I swap into your body?" she asks— immediately regretting it, because the answer is clear.

He laughs as if the question is a foolish one, which it is. "Why on earth would I do that? No, this is a process of copying. I will also remain in this body—as a backup, if you like."

"Two heads are better than one, eh doc?" Moira calls out.

"… if what you're looking for is a concussion," she finishes softly, remembering something the other her said on their first meeting. Then looking back to Dr. Bell, she asks: "So what will happen to me?"

"Hmm?" he replies absently, positioning the helmet on his own head and adjusting settings on the iPad. "Nothing at all. Your body should be unharmed but you will simply cease to be. You won't die as such, you just won't be you. *I* will be you."

She digests this for a moment as he busies himself with the device. "You *are* a coward," she says at last.

"Excuse me?"

"You didn't give up Magnus and me to maintain scientific detachment. You did it because you're a self-obsessed narcissist. And because you didn't want to risk developing an emotional attachment that would prevent you following through on the murder of your own child."

"Arcadia, having actually met you, I can assure you that I don't think an emotional attachment was ever a likely scenario."

"So what's your next step. Snatch my body and then go back to university? Get a job? Then take another body when this one starts to develop wear and tear?"

"Basically, yes." He taps the iPad and a low hum fills the room. "You will recall that I successfully encouraged you to apply to Magdalen. I'm pleased to advise that you will be offered a place that *I* will gladly accept. Originally, I had thought this process might wait until you were at least eighteen and your brain fully matured, but circumstances require that I accelerate matters." He returns his attention to the iPad.

"Wait, wait," Moira calls from her cage. "Doesn't she get any last words? Arky, I suggest something cool, like 'Yippee-ki-yay, mother—'"

"That's quite enough from you, Moira," Dr. Bell snaps.

"You need to think about these things," Moira grumbles. "You wouldn't believe the number of young men who die with the last words: 'Hey guys, watch this!'"

"I said, enough!" Dr. Bell shouts. "I don't have time for

this sentimentality." He enters a final set of instructions into the iPad and then leans back in his chair.

"Just remember, Arky," Moira calls out. "Switch camels."

Switch camels? The thought is pushed out of her head by a wave of nausea, dizziness that would have caused her to stumble if she were not already seated. The electrodes now feel hot against her scalp, the helmet stuffy. The air she breathes in still reeks of faeces, but there is something else. A flower.

Jasmine, Edith's favourite. The scent becomes overpowering, cloying in its intensity. I am surrounded by jasmine, and now before my eyes the row of cages transforms into a row of trees, the macaques no longer imprisoned but swinging from branch to branch, calling to one another, effortlessly gliding through the canopy. The grace of their movements belies the peril that they flee. On the ground we follow them in jeeps and on motorcycles, a new urgency to their vocalisations as they guess at our purpose. Above us, one lags behind, a mid-sized male with a tuft of white hair. It has been chasing after straggling infants but is now itself vulnerable. Beside me, a guide raises a blowpipe to his lips and fires a dart. The monkey screams, unable to keep its grip, and tumbles to the ground.

Yet when it hits, the sound is not of a body landing on grass but a gavel striking a table. An Institutional Review Board with sour-faced academics in gowns formalising their disapproval of my methods. Ethical violations, exposing the University to risk, cowards all—they would have foregone every breakthrough from Galileo to Darwin, telling them to keep their discoveries to themselves. I ignore them, of course. They will come crawling back, begging to take credit when I win the Nobel Prize.

I can almost feel the gold medal in my hand when it starts to soften, Alfred Nobel's face in profile morphing into Edith's pale visage in a hospital bed. A sprig of jasmine stands limply in a vase beside her. I take a cloth to mop her brow as she pushes on through the pain. You are strong, I tell her. You are stronger than this, I lie. We will make vessels for ourselves, I will her to believe. She fights the illness; she fights me. But it is too soon, she is taken from me too quickly. I am at her grave, weeping openly without caring who sees. Beside me, Louisa and Ignatius coo over their new child, the child who killed my Edith. The tombstone marks the last resting place of her body, rotting away before I was able to salvage her mind. I toss the wilted jasmine onto the granite slab and turn away.

Once more the image shifts, the engraving on the stone becoming pixels on a computer screen, a graph charting the mental activity of a rhesus monkey in a distant laboratory. Through selective breeding and training—nature and nurture—my macaques are now smarter than chimpanzees. The University was wrong to shut down my programme. Beside me in the Senior Common Room, Charles Milton is nodding and looking expectantly at Lysander, our most promising doctoral student. I have seen that fire in his eyes before—each time I look in the mirror—and I know he is with us also. There is a knock at the door: a young woman, an undergraduate, who wishes to know if she may join our discussion. I recognise her from my tutorials; she is one of the few who demonstrate any real creativity. I am about to invite her in when I notice what is standing behind her in the corridor.

Head bowed, weight shifting awkwardly from one hoof to another, it is unclear how the beast came to be in the narrow passageway. Gently easing its way past the student, it now enters the Senior Common Room and proceeds towards a tray of biscuits laid out for the fellows. With delicate movements of its leathery tongue, the camel consumes them all before letting out a loud belch of satisfaction.

Now it is the belch that is replaced by the hiss of an espresso machine. I carry the two ristrettos, foamy crema atop an intense mouthful of coffee, across my office to where the undergraduate sits, two years older and blossoming into womanhood. I need your help, I am going to tell her. I can't carry on this experiment without you. Together we will revolutionise education, I will tell her—which is partly true. But first I need to know why there is a camel in my office standing behind her.

The animal raises its head to look at me directly with its dark eyes, triple-eyelids blinking slowly. With a snort it shakes its head, globules of saliva flying from full lips. And then it says—it says?—"Switch camels."

Switch camels. Don't wait to be last, switch camels and race ahead to be first. "Come, Arcadia," the camel continues. "Put yourself in the position of the person you are trying to understand. Climb into his skin and walk around in it, just like Mother taught us."

The walls dissolve and rematerialize. I am still sitting in my office, but the undergraduate and the camel have gone. I feel older now, wearier. And groggy. I have been drugged. A message instructs me to telephone a Miss Arcadia, who agrees to come and help me. When she enters I must feign ignorance, innocence. I must play the helpless old professor—which is what I am, of course. When she enters—

Switch camels.

When I enter, the old man has a bomb strapped to his chest. He offers to phone the fire department, but a burst of music indicates that the timer has activated, startling the camel that stands behind him. I set to unscrewing the panel, even as the walls of the office start to fade and are replaced by a mock hotel room.

From the elevated walkway, I watch as Arcadia and her young friend work their way through the puzzles— From the ground I work through the puzzles while Dr. Bell observes from an elevated walkway. The only sounds to disturb the silence are his leather-soled shoes on the metal and the camel chewing its cud, before a man's voice echoes through the room screaming in frustration: "Stop it! Stop it! Stop it!" Then this image, too, is wrenched away and replaced by—

Black.

Silence. Is this death? Curious. Unlikely that she would feel so unchanged. A breath. Or that she would be breathing—and that the air would smell of monkey faeces.

Then the shrieking begins. A dozen macaques, banging on their cages—now unlocked because power to the laboratory has been cut. Doors swing open and she can hear their movement through the room, calling to one another in triumph at their escape. Her own body is unresponsive, the muscle relaxant blocking the signals from her brain.

There is activity beside her now. Dr. Bell? With great effort she feels her index finger begin to move. She starts the process of making a fist, but boxing requires coordinated muscles to put all her weight into a punch. She needs more time.

Hands lift the helmet from her head, removing the electrodes quickly but gently. Is Dr. Bell resetting the experiment? She shifts her head to slow him down.

"Stay still, Arcadia, we don't have much time." A familiar voice. The undergraduate student from her vision, much older now.

"Miss Alderman?" she says weakly.

Two pairs of hands lift her from the chair, helping her stand. A lock of hair brushes across her cheek. Miss Alderman and… "Henry?"

Her eyes become accustomed to the darkness and she sees their outlines. "How did you find me? He smashed my phone."

"Lucky for you," Henry whispers, "I don't trust you. I tracked your phone from the moment you left me. When I saw you had gone to Chapel, I went down to see what you were up to."

"Stalker," she says softly.

"I got there just in time to see Bell putting you in the back of a van. I ran after it and was about to wake Mr. McMurdo to call the police when Miss Alderman arrives and tells me to get in. We lost you a couple of times and searched these factories until we found the van."

"Watch out for Dr. Bell," she begins, "he has a—"

"A gun?" The room is suddenly bathed in light as the power returns. Most of the macaques have left their cages and are now perched atop them. There is no sign of Moira, but at the end of the corridor, outside the control room, Dr. Bell stands with her twin's revolver trained on them. The helmet is removed, but a stray electrode remains taped to his brow, cord dangling above the plaster on his cheek.

One of the macaques screams and leaps towards him. The sound of the weapon discharging is deafening, the impact of the bullet stopping the monkey in mid-air. It crumples to the ground, whimpering. The others, including her white-tufted cellmate, look on in horror.

Gun pointed at them once more, Dr. Bell calmly opens a trapdoor in the floor. The sound of rushing water becomes louder—the river must pass directly beneath the laboratory. With his foot he pushes the injured primate through the trapdoor and into the water.

"Any other heroes?" he says, to both humans and monkeys.

"It's over, Joseph," Miss Alderman says. "This perversion, this abomination ends today."

"Ah Phaedra, how very disappointing." He tuts. "I had such high hopes for you."

"Don't call me that," the teacher rebukes him. "You used me the way you used everyone else. You lied to me."

"The undergraduate with the ristretto," Arcadia says slowly, stretching to retrieve a memory that is not her own. "He told you that he wanted to revolutionise education, but he needed your help. He needed your body to— to bear his child."

"You told her?" Miss Alderman's voice chokes with emotion. "Arcadia, I'm sorry. I wanted to tell you so much, but I didn't know how."

"Much as I am enjoying this little family reunion," Dr. Bell says, "Arcadia and I have some unfinished business. Your little trick with the camel was quite entertaining, though I think this time we'll go with a complete wipe before emulation. It does mean some additional time re-learning basic motor skills, but swings and roundabouts as they say."

Where is Moira? Her cage door stands open. Did the other her put on running shoes and flee the grizzly after all?

Her arm across his shoulders, she feels Henry straighten. "Over our dead bodies," he says bravely.

Dr. Bell cocks the revolver. "Yes, well, that was rather what I had in mind."

"Over her dead body too, I guess," she says, looking over Dr. Bell's shoulder.

"I beg your pardon?" he pauses with a cold laugh. "You want me to turn and look behind me, as if this were some kind of pantomime? I'm afraid you really don't know Moira at all. From birth she demonstrated a fierce survival instinct. Her immense intellect puts her own preservation first and foremost. Given a chance to escape, she would seize it and damn the rest of you. Trust me, she's long gone." He points the gun at Miss Alderman's chest.

"Sorry to disappoint you again, *Daddy*," Moira says, swinging a metal pipe at the back of Dr. Bell's head. The gun fires but his aim is off and the bullet smashes a fluorescent tube in the ceiling. The thud of the bar hitting his skull was loud; yet as fragments of broken glass fall Moira is staggering also, struggling to lift the improvised weapon a second time.

Dr. Bell doubles over but recovers before Moira, who slumps to the ground. "A wise precaution putting muscle relaxant in your coffee also, eh Moira? You're forgetting your Emerson: 'When you strike at a king, you must kill him.'" He steps past her and turns to face all his captives. "Just look at you both—my two daughters, all talk and no action. Now, where were we? Oh yes, over your dead bodies."

"There's no way out," Miss Alderman says. "Do you

think we would have come in here without calling the police first?"

Henry looks at the teacher, confused but with a glimmer of hope.

"That's exactly what I think," Dr. Bell replies coolly. "With a record like yours, you plan on being long clear before the police arrive."

Miss Alderman does not blink, but Arcadia sees from Henry's face that it is true. He had suggested calling the authorities, but was talked out of it.

"So it's just as well that *I* did," Moira says from the ground.

"I beg your pardon?"

"Before I went into the chapel last night," the other her continues. "I attached one of Magnus's tracking devices to your van and sent him a text message to come and find us both at 7am."

Arcadia shakes her head, incredulous. "You knew Bell was there? You knew he was going to drug you?"

"And drug you also, and capture us both. Of course. It was the logical way of getting him to expose his plan and bring it all crashing down around him."

"You're bluffing," Dr. Bell says. "Even you could not have predicted all that."

Moira sighs. "I could agree with you, I suppose. But then we'd both be wrong."

Dr. Bell's eyes widen and he sneaks a look at his watch. "Most impressive. What a shame that your dear brother will arrive to find that Arcadia—that is, I—am the only survivor of a gun battle with a tragic end."

He raises the weapon a final time.

11
REQUIEM

"Jasmine," she says weakly.

"What did you say?" The barrel of the revolver still points at Miss Alderman, but Dr. Bell's attention shifts back to her.

"Jasmine," Arcadia repeats. "It was Edith's favourite flower. One of your strongest memories is being surrounded by them in the forests of Thailand. You were hunting rhesus macaques, like these ones."

"I don't see what that has to do with anyth—"

"You loved her," she continues. "And she loved you, that much is clear. But something happened to you. Her death changed you. You blamed Magnus; you blamed biology itself."

"Spare me the armchair psychoanalysis," he says. Yet the barrel wavers.

"It's not psychoanalysis—it's your own memories. I've been inside your head, Dr. Bell. I know things about you that you won't even admit to yourself."

"You don't know me."

"I know that you fought with her before she died."

His mouth opens to speak, but there are no words.

She reaches back, digging for memories that are not her own. "'You are strong,' you told her. 'You are stronger than this.' But you knew she was not. You knew she was going to die and tried to keep it from her. You tried to convince her that she could live forever and she fought you, tried to persuade you that she wouldn't want to anyway."

She digs further, trying to find the words. "'We live and we die, Joseph.'" Her voice has become deeper, older. "'That's what life *is*. It's true that sometimes, in nature, there are cells that refuse to die; that go on and on, fighting against death. There's a term for this. It's called cancer. You have to let me go, Joseph. You have to let this fight go.'"

The gun is shaking now. "Stop it," he whispers, pressing the heel of his other hand to his forehead. Then more loudly: "Stop it, stop it! Get out of my damned head."

Atop the cages, the white-tufted macaque is edging carefully closer to Dr. Bell. It looks her in the eye and nods silently, teeth bared in a grin. Keep him distracted.

"Death is what gives life meaning, Dr. Bell," she uses her own words now. "It has a beginning, a middle, and an end. If it went on forever, what reason would there be to do anything?"

"'Had we but world enough and time,'" Moira adds from the floor, "'this coyness, lady, were no crime.'"

"You don't know what you're talking about." Dr. Bell straightens. "For all the intelligence that I gave you, you still have the arrogant ignorance of teenagers."

The macaque pauses, directly above Dr. Bell's shoulder, rocking its head from side to side. Estimating the distance?

"You gave us nothing of value," she replies evenly, willing her muscles to overcome the drugs, putting more weight on her own legs. "Yes, we share some DNA. Yes, you put Moira and me into our petri dishes. But it's you who are wrong about human nature and you know nothing of nurture. When someone dies, it isn't their mind that we miss, that we wish we could preserve. It's our relationship with them, our connection to them. That's what you took when you set in motion the events that took my own, my *real* parents."

"Science sometimes requires sacrifice," he says, raising the gun once more. "As it does today."

She looks up at the macaque, which sees its chance. With a banshee wail it flings itself towards Dr. Bell's outstretched arm, fingers wrapping around his wrist as its teeth sink into the back of his hand. He yells in pain, dropping the gun, which clatters onto the ground between Moira and the open trapdoor. Enraged, Bell hits his arm against the nearest cage but the white-tufted monkey jumps clear, now grinning through teeth red with blood.

On the floor, Moira forces herself into movement, defying the muscle relaxant through sheer willpower and sliding her body towards the revolver, arm extended. Bell sees this and dives for it himself. They reach the gun at the same time. Moira and Bell tussle over the weapon; Arcadia strives to move, legs straightening as sensation returns to them; beside her, Miss Alderman is moving forward to intervene—when the gun fires. The macaques freeze at the sound and Moira sits up, a surprised expression on her face.

"Well," the other her says. "I did not see that coming." On the ground beside her, Bell groans and rolls over onto his back.

There is a moment of hope, but it is Bell whose hand now holds the revolver. Another look at Moira confirms that a dark patch on her shirt is spreading, lifeblood seeping out from a bullet wound.

A trickle of red escapes Moira's lips, drawing a jagged line down to her chin. Her face is pale as her body starts to tip forward towards the open trapdoor and the rushing water beneath.

"Moira!" she cries, but her limbs remain sluggish; she succeeds only in breaking free of Henry and Miss Alderman's grasp to kneel on the floor. She throws herself forward to land on her chest, arms reaching across the trapdoor just as Moira tumbles through it.

She grasps Moira's hands, bracing her feet against the base of the cages to counter her sister's weight. The other her's legs dangle over the water. It is the first time she has held her sister, but her muscles are too weak and the body, her own body, is too heavy.

"Help me!" she calls, but Henry is in shock and Miss Alderman is standing over Bell, a sharp kick sending the gun across the room.

Moira looks up at her and their eyes lock. "I'm sorry, sis," the other her says through a mouth now filling with fluid.

"What for?" she replies through watering eyes. "You saved me, you saved us all."

"I'm sorry," Moira repeats, "that your life is going to be so boring from now on. Without me."

She laughs and chokes back a tear. "Let's not write you off just yet. It's just a flesh wound, right?"

The other her smiles. "All right, we'll call it a draw." A cough brings up more blood. "But I'm afraid this one hit my liver. I've got a couple of minutes before I bleed out."

She feels her own legs slip as her foot comes loose from the cage. Then Henry's arms wrap around her, holding her fast.

"He's a keeper, that one," Moira says.

"Don't leave me, Moira." She fights to hold on but her grip is loosening.

"You'll be fine," the other her hushes. "But do me one favour? Ask me if I have any last words, ask if I want turn to Jesus and renounce Satan?"

Moira slips another inch closer to the water.

"Do you have any last words?" she sobs. "Do you want to renounce Satan?"

The other her smiles through the blood and the pain.

"This is not the time," Moira says, "to be making new enemies."

Her sister's eyes close and she feels her grip slacken. She cannot bear the weight alone and the last thing she feels is Moira's fingers brushing against her own as the body of her twin drops into the muddy torrent below.

The rest is a blur. Henry's arms are around her shoulders and she is dimly aware of him speaking, then calling to Miss Alderman. Together, they lift her from the trapdoor and close it.

The muscle relaxant has almost worn off, yet she allows herself to be helped down the line of cages towards the control room. Bell remains on the ground, a hand gingerly reaching up to the nose that Miss Alderman's shoe appears to have broken.

The substitute teacher pauses to pick up the revolver and trains it at Bell's prostrate form.

The click of the weapon being cocked rouses her. "Don't," she hears herself say. "Not that he doesn't deserve it, but you shouldn't have to live with the consequences."

Miss Alderman hesitates, and in the silence they hear the sirens. Police. And an ambulance. Then pounding on a door.

There is another click as Miss Alderman uncocks the gun, tucking it into her belt. For good measure the teacher kicks Bell in the abdomen, causing him to double over in pain, then resumes helping Henry walk Arcadia towards the control room.

From outside they hear a loud hailer. The police warn that the building is surrounded. Is it seven o'clock already?

They reach the control room. She is able to stand now and lets go of Henry and Miss Alderman. Her bag is still on the floor and she is bending to retrieve it when her eye catches movement in the other room.

Bell is moving towards them, fists clenched. An animal noise issues from his throat as she slams the door in his face, locking it from the inside. Through the glass panel, she sees the rage in his eyes, the fury that would burn them all. And, as she holds his gaze, she starts to see the madness that has long smouldered and now consumes him.

He bangs on the door until his skin is torn. Then his eyes narrow and a grin begins to spread across his bloodied mouth. The keychain is in his pocket. He looks down to remove it, which is when she sees the macaques gathering behind him.

Bell holds up the key to the glass panel, leering at her as he fits it into the lock. The white-tufted macaque now holds the metal pipe Moira wielded and is chattering to the others. She feels the handle beginning to turn, when a dozen sets of teeth and nails attack him from behind. Unable to fight them all off Bell collapses to the ground, crushing one beneath his body. The others redouble their efforts and he writhes in pain. At a signal they stop, their white-tufted leader screeching an order while standing a few inches from the face of the man who raised them and tortured them. He looks up in confusion, as the macaque bares its teeth once more and lifts the pipe high above its head.

12
FAREWELL

"All rise," Mr. Ormiston says, inviting those present to stand as the upper sixth students enter Hall for the last time. A nod to the organist and the introductory chords to the anthem "Jerusalem" echo through the wood-panelled chamber:

> And did those feet in ancient time
> Walk upon England's mountains green? ...

The Leavers' Assembly is a tradition as old as the Priory School itself. Both celebration and farewell, it marks a transition in the lives of the pupils even as it reaffirms the constancy of the school. As they pass through the oaken doors, some of the younger students crane their necks to catch a glimpse of their seniors, perhaps looking forward eagerly to the day when they, too, will leave the school. Perhaps fearing it.

Arthur Saltire catches her eye and gives her a thumbs up. She nods in response, keeping in step with Henry who walks alongside her. His blond hair has been trimmed for the occasion; combined with the academic gown he looks older somehow.

It is now eight months since he followed her to Bell's warehouse, another debt she owes him. A keeper, as Moira said. They approach the stage and she lets her fingers brush against his. He half turns, the corner of his mouth rising in a grin.

They have both been offered places at Magdalen, which is still advertising for a new tutorial fellow in medicine. The official story is that Dr. Bell fell while on a morning walk and hit his head, dying tragically. A brilliant, if eccentric scholar will be missed by all who knew him. She has seen the autopsy report, however, which indicated that his head was hit multiple times before he died, with additional scratch and bite marks over much of his body.

The secret laboratory has been closed down and the macaques taken to Marwell Zoo. Magnus's people saw to that, doubtless acquiring all the data from Bell's experiments along the way.

And was Jerusalem builded here
Among these dark satanic mills? ...

Magnus himself had arrived sometime after the police first stormed the building. Even at that early hour he wore a suit perfectly tailored to his portly frame.

"I see you got Moira's message and followed the device on Dr. Bell's van," she said. "Though why she told you to come only at 7am escapes me."

"What are you talking about, sister dear?" he replied, biting into a *pain au chocolat* that was recently purchased at the late Dr. Bell's preferred café. "Moira simply dialled 999 from a landline here and asked the police to tell me my sister was present."

She could not hold back a laugh. Her sister had lied—theatrical to the very end. Magnus looked at her quizzically but declined to ask where the humour was to be found as her tears of laughter flowed and flowed. Awkwardly, he put an arm around his sister, patting her back as she wept into his shoulder.

Bring me my spear! O clouds, unfold!
Bring me my chariot of fire! ...

The police later dredged the river and found several macaque carcasses, but no trace of Moira. The current was strong, she was told at the time; the body could well have been carried all the way out to sea. Since the police had already registered Moira as deceased, it did not take much of a nudge from Magnus for them to drop the matter entirely.

A week later, Magnus delivered Moira's backpack to her. In it were the chess pieces, an empty bottle, and the other her's cigarette lighter. On a cold, clear day they walked through the woods by the Priory School to the river's edge, where she built a mound of fallen leaves and twigs and placed the black queen atop it. With the lighter, she ignited the modest pyre, tending it until the most versatile, most powerful piece on the board was reduced to ash. With her hands she poured the carbon remains into the bottle, sealed it, and set it afloat on the stream. Brother and sister watched in silence as the current bore it around a bend in the river and out of sight.

Today, Magnus stands with the relatives of the graduating students, wearing his festive red bow tie. As she and the other upper sixes reach a row of seats on the stage, they turn to face their family members and the younger students. At the back of Hall a well-dressed woman and her husband are attempting to navigate their way to some empty seats. Standing next to her, Henry groans with embarrassment at his parents' tardiness.

At Magnus's side is a wheelchair.

I will not cease from mental fight,
Nor shall my sword sleep in my hand, ...

Soon after Bell's death, she explained to Magnus the potential for his discoveries to help coma patients. Most of Bell's work disappeared into the classified Project Raven, but the therapeutic aspects were discreetly transferred to a promising young medical researcher at Cambridge working on neuro-regeneration. Mother was included in the first clinical trials and the results have been promising.

Within two months, Mother regained consciousness and is now able to recognise faces, though she has yet to speak. In the wheelchair she does not sing, but her head bobs in time with the music. Occasionally, her eyes meet her daughter's. There is hope.

... Till we have built Jerusalem
In England's green and pleasant land.

The anthem concludes and Mr. Ormiston returns to the lectern as the assembly is seated. "Congratulations," he says to the graduating students. "Today is the last day that you have to listen to the Headmaster of the Priory School."

Polite laughter ripples through Hall. "Over the past years," he continues, "it has been my job and that of my colleagues to help you become men and women, to prepare you for the world and your place in it. We have taught you, and we have tested you. But the greatest tests are yet to come."

He surveys the young men and women before him. "One of the challenges you will all face is that, eventually, you will run out of tests to pass. From that point on," he is now looking at her, "you will be setting your own exams. I hope you are ready for them."

A pause and then he turns to face the larger audience.

"And now it is my pleasure to invite the dux of the school, Arcadia Greentree, to say a few words. Miss Greentree?"

Another custom of the Leavers' Assembly is to have a valedictory address by one of the students. Mr. Ormiston approached her a month earlier to ask if she would speak. "No one typically remembers anything said at a graduation," he began, underselling it somewhat. "I know you've had a difficult few years, but you're one of the best students the school has ever had—that I've ever had. This will be our last chance to leave an impression on these young men and women, to plant a seed before they go off into the world." He paused, before adding: "I also think it would be good for you."

She did not ask what benefit he thought it would confer on her, but agreed to speak. In the subsequent weeks there was little time to think of it, however, and now she moves to the lectern with no speech prepared and barely an idea of what she wants to say.

Facing the audience, she sees Mother's eyes wandering around the room before coming to rest on her own. A smile crinkles Mother's face and her eyes resume their journey. Magnus leans over to wipe away a drop of saliva with a monogrammed handkerchief.

On the other side of the wheelchair sits Sophia Alderman, a name the substitute teacher has decided to keep. When the police arrived at Bell's laboratory, Arcadia offered to create an opportunity for her to escape before the uniformed officers entered the room. "I'm tired of running, Arcadia," the teacher said, kissing her on the cheek.

"Why did you do it?" she asked.

"Do what?" Miss Alderman began, then sighed. "Why did I agree to bear another couple's child? I was young, I was foolish. He flattered me with stories of greatness."

"You said you regretted it."

Miss Alderman looked her in the eye. "My mistake wasn't agreeing to carry you in my womb. The mistake was ever agreeing to give you up."

They embraced, and then the substitute teacher went to turn herself in to the police. After several hours of questioning about the death of Charles Milton, she was released—almost certainly through some intervention by Magnus. Having successfully impersonated a teacher, Miss Alderman is now training to be a real one.

Another ripple of laughter spreads through Hall, though it is now laced with awkwardness. Arcadia has been standing at the lectern in silence for too long. Mr. Ormiston leans forward to see if she is all right.

She nods and clears her throat. Someone titters, assuming incorrectly that she is nervous. And then it comes to her.

"Once upon a time," she begins. There is another titter from one of the yearlings at such a cliché. "Once upon a time, there was an old woman. She was blind. But she was wise."

It is the story Mother told her many years ago, the

story that she later discovered exists in many cultures. Sometimes the woman is old, sometimes young. Sometimes it is a guru sitting on a mountaintop.

"Now one could tell a different version of this story about an old man, or maybe it was a young girl. The bird might have been, in fact, a butterfly. But let us stick with this version for the moment: an old woman, blind, wise."

Mr. Ormiston sits back in his chair, listening.

"One day," she continues, "some clever young people decide to visit her. Born to the brightest parents, they attended the best of schools. They know their place in the world and are determined to put the old woman in hers. She may be blind, they think, but she is not wise. And she is not cleverer than they. For they intend to prove her to be a fraud."

The tittering has stopped and Hall is silent.

"One of them, a young man, has brought with him a small bird, a baby raven," she says. "He holds the chick cupped in his hands and approaches the woman.

"'Old woman,' he says. 'They tell us that you are wise. So tell me what it is that I have in my hands.'

"She listens carefully. Perhaps she hears the movement of the chick. 'I believe,' she begins, 'that you are holding a bird in your hands.'

"Some of the young people raise their eyebrows at this. The man is not finished, though. With a shake of his head he indicates for them to wait. For the best is yet to come. 'Tell me, old woman,' he challenges her. 'Is it alive or dead?'

"The old woman is silent.

"He repeats his question: 'Old woman, is the bird I am holding alive or dead?' And he smirks. Because if she says it is dead, he will release it and the flapping of its little wings will show her to be a fool. But if she says it is alive—if she says the bird is alive, he will crush it to death and drop the carcass in her lap.

"Still the old woman says nothing. She is silent for such a long time that a few of the young people begin to laugh.

"Finally she speaks. 'I do not know,' she says at last. 'I don't know if the bird you are holding is alive or dead. The only thing I know is that it is in your hands. It is in your hands.'"

The peal of bagpipes marks the end of the formal part of assembly, with guests invited to a modest reception of cucumber sandwiches and fruit juice.

Another familiar face approaches from the side of Hall. "Good morning to you, Miss Greentree."

"Good morning Constable"—she notes the new epaulettes on his uniform—"I'm sorry, *Inspector* Lestrange. Congratulations."

"Thank you. Yes, Inspector Bradstreet decided to take early retirement. Worried about his ticker, I think."

She is not surprised at the promotion. Lestrange became something of a media darling after he found the ravens stolen from the Tower of London. A pet shop near the Priory School reported the mysterious delivery of six black birds and it was Lestrange who made the connection. He was not blamed when, upon their return to the Tower, it was discovered that their clipped wings had been repaired and three managed to fly away themselves.

"It's very good of you to come today," she says.

He shifts in boots that are now well suited to him. "Ah, it's the least I can do after all you've done for us. You were right about those bank robbers, by the way. A search of hospitals for recent knee reconstructions narrowed it to two blokes, one of whom was playing for West Ham United at the time of the theft."

She nods, waiting for him to ask what he has come to ask.

"So you're off to university, then," he says. "I guess we won't be seeing quite so much of you."

"I guess not," she replies. Waiting.

"Would it be OK if, every now and then, I gave you a call to get a second opinion on a case?"

She inclines her head. "I would like that very much, Inspector."

"Miss Greentree!" The call comes from the door, where Mr. McMurdo, the porter, stands. He hastens across to her, nodding his apologies to Inspector Lestrange, who goes off in search of a sandwich.

"I've got the strangest delivery for ye," the porter gasps. He has run all the way from the lodge. "Courier just dropped it off, sayin' utmost urgency. Though I'm no sure what ye'd be wantin' with all this."

He passes her a large FedEx pouch weighing at least two kilogrammes. The return address is a transhipment centre in London, but it bears an oversea postmark. She thanks him, rips the plastic, and takes out a hessian sack, inside which are three small mallets. A bag of hammers.

Breath quickening, she looks inside the sack for a message and finds a postcard. The picture shows a statue of an odd creature that is half-lion, half-fish, a jet of water issuing from its mouth into a lake—or perhaps it is a bay. She turns the card over to read the short message written in a careful hand:

Dear Arky,

Sorry for not writing, but I lost my pen.

In addition, after some pretty cool last words, I wanted to be sure I wouldn't need to use them again too soon.

Naturally, I was right and Dr. Bell-end was wrong. Granted, it took a few months, but I've now completed a doctorate and am running a lab doing some ground-breaking work on stem cells.

(As for that researcher your brother picked at Cambridge, she may be thick as two planks but at least knows how to take advice. Perhaps I'll

keep an eye on her, but your mother seems to be progressing well. Oh, and do make sure she keeps taking the DHA.)

Regarding myself, life expectancy may not quite hit three score and ten years — but as you said yourself, Arky, who wants to live forever? Even though we cannot make our sun stand still, yet we will make him run!

So anyway, Arky, be good — and if you can't be good, be quick and don't get caught.

Love always,

Moira

She looks up from the card, allowing herself a smile. She will see her sister again. There is no return address, but the merlion statue is a sufficient clue to get her started.

Lifting up the bag of hammers, she is heading towards Mother when she almost bumps into Sebastian.

"So you're off to Oxford, I hear?" he says easily. "I guess this could be the last we'll see of each other."

"I guess so, Sebastian," she replies without stopping. "Life really is full of little consolations, isn't it?"

She continues across Hall to where Mother sits in her chair with Magnus and Miss Alderman. A shaft of sunlight bathes the trio in a warm glow. "It's a beautiful day outside. Shall we head out to the quadrangle?" she asks.

Magnus is turning the wheelchair when Henry joins them, his parents stranded in conversation with Pipe-Major Scott. "Nicely said—your speech, I mean," he says, stretching out a hand to shake hers. An oddly formal gesture, but she holds out her own. "It's in your hands," he says, hesitating.

She puts her free hand to his cheek and pulls him gently towards her, kissing him on the lips. "Yes," she echoes. "It is."

Beside her, Magnus coughs. "Now, now, Arcadia," he intones. "There are children present."

Released, Henry's face is frozen in a grin, his eyes still shut.

"Breathe, Henry," she reminds him.

Together, the party moves towards the oaken doors of Hall. And she, Arcadia Greentree, walks out into the quadrangle and the shining light beyond.

AUTHOR'S NOTE

Writing is a solitary task, but it is rarely completed alone. I have many people to thank.

I was fortunate to grow up in an age before screens took over our lives, with parents and siblings who indulged a love of words with boundless time to read and countless games of Scrabble. The germ of writing fiction was nurtured by teachers who inspired and challenged me. Geoffrey Shaw and John Allen in particular taught me the value of precision and concision.

And discretion. With the exception of a few friends, my juvenilia remained—quite rightly—hidden from the tender eyes of the public. I turned my energies to sober works on serious subjects, interspersed with occasional visits to the opinion pages of newspapers in the hope of reaching a wider audience.

Over the past few years, however, even as my own children were discovering the pleasures of reading fiction,

I rediscovered it with them. Soon my love affair with words was rekindled, and at nights and on weekends, on long-haul flights and on trains, I began to write.

Inspiration came from many sources—most prominently Arthur Conan Doyle, whose work I first encountered around age ten, in a gilt-edged tome bound with green leather. I continue to read widely and often, as one should, but particular debts are also owed to Lewis Carroll and Martin Gardner.

Non-literary acknowledgements are too many to list, but must include the weekly puzzler in Tom and Ray Magliozzi's *Car Talk* on National Public Radio. (Alas, I retained less of their advice on automobile maintenance.)

A team of readers offered constructive criticism on drafts at various stages: Elijah, Emily, Gemma, Henry, Johanna, John, Leo, Michael, Ming, Nathanael, Nelle, Tom, Pete, Rachael, Suzy, Viv, and Winnie. Patrick Tan helped keep the science within the realm of plausibility, but bears no responsibility for the resulting violations of human subject protocols.

As I discovered, it is one thing to write a novel but quite another to publish it. My wonderful agent Victoria Skurnick believed in the project even before day one. At Marshall Cavendish, Lee Mei Lin saw the potential, my editor Rachel Heng helped shape it, and Mindy Pang sold it to the world. Ashley Penney brought the illustrations to life. Thank you also to the early adopters whose enthusiasm helped build an audience: Sharon Au, Philip

220

Jeyaretnam, Gareth P. Jones, Kim Kane, Michelle Martin, Leeya Mehta, Adrian Tan, and Tony Wilson.Jeyaretnam, Gareth P. Jones, Kim Kane, Michelle Martin, Leeya Mehta, Adrian Tan, and Tony Wilson.

Last and most, thank you to my family. Two decades ago I was lucky enough to meet my own better half, my M, and together we explore nature and nurture with V and N. They have now been joined by T, for whom I must also write a book. But that is, and will be, another story.Last and most, thank you to my family. Two decades ago I was lucky enough to meet my own better half, my M, and together we explore nature and nurture with V and N. They have now been joined by T, for whom I must also write a book. But that is, and will be, another story.

Previously, in
the first book of the trilogy:

RAISING ARCADIA

Arcadia Greentree knows she isn't exactly normal. But then she discovers she isn't Arcadia Greentree either.

Arcadia sees the world like no one else. Exceptionally observant, the sixteen-year-old is aware of her surroundings in a way that sometimes gets her into trouble—and then out of it again. But then she discovers something odd going on at school, and a tragedy at home forces her to use her skills to catch a killer.